MS DEE

MS DEEDES AT HOME

Carole Andrews

Nexus

First published in Great Britain in 1992 by
Nexus
338 Ladbroke Grove
London W10 5AH

Copyright © Carole Andrews 1992

ISBN 0 352 32824 X

Phototypeset by Intype, London
Printed and bound in Great Britain by
Cox & Wyman Ltd, Reading, Berks.

This book is sold subject to the condition that it shall not, by way of trade or otherwise, be lent, resold, hired out or otherwise circulated without the publisher's prior written consent in any form of binding or cover other than that in which it is published and without a similar condition including this condition being imposed on the subsequent purchaser.

CONTENTS

1	The Banishment	1
2	Not Quite Cricket	14
3	All Well and Good	28
4	On the Beaten Path	47
5	Déjeuner sur l'Herbe	63
6	All Well and Goode	78
7	Applied Mechanics	97
8	Taking the Rough with the Smooth	111
9	Ding Dong Bell	124
10	One Flower Makes No Garland	137
11	Fêteful Ambition	149
12	Interstellar Overdrive	162
13	To Each Their Isle	176

Enjoy this exciting read. But when you have sex, make sure you practise *safer* sex.

Carole Andrews

1

THE BANISHMENT

It was her turn next. She couldn't believe the cheek of him, making her wait outside his office like a naughty schoolgirl. She scanned the faces of his clients, waiting on the bench beside her. They looked guilty. They looked worried about how much he was going to charge. They looked frightened. But she wasn't in awe of him, she told herself.

'Ms Deedes?'

She entered the outer office, which was clerical and plastic. It was dominated by computer consoles, display screens and an austere secretary in horn-rimmed glasses.

'He will see you now, Ms Deedes.'

'You bet he will. And hear me, too. I've been a golden little girl for the past six months and he summons me here like a criminal!' She barged through into the inner sanctum, with its plush suede armchairs and walls lined with leather-bound legal books.

'Hello, Ella. I'm sending you back home.'

'Home?' She froze for a moment, as though unable to trust her ears. Then the wind went out of her with a deep sigh of relief. 'My guardian angel!' And she leaned forward over his wide desk and kissed his forehead.

'Not home to New York, Ella. I mean all the way back home. Home to England.'

The premature smile of gratitude vanished at once from her face as her guardian angel became again simply, but infuriatingly, her guardian.

Eleanor Deedes was indeed English, and was possessed by the same zest for life in all its physical and earthy glory which had been her mother's great appeal. When the desert-dry Texan industrialist Kirk Deedes had fallen under the spell of that earlier English rose, picked her, and brought her to America for his buttonhole, he had been obliged also to bring with him the tiny bud which was her two-year-old daughter Eleanor. The mature rose shrivelled and died, its zest for life cruelly perverted on a feed of alcohol and closet drugs, and the little bud became a thorny, uncared-for problem.

Hence the guardian. Ella was not on first-name terms with him. At twenty-three she was now a full-blown rose herself, past awkward May and into the glorious sun-kissed June of her life. But still she was controlled, the generous allowance which supported her rich taste for life metered out in return for her compliance with certain rules – no pestering, no gossip and above all, no scandal.

'But I've done nothing wrong at all! Look at me!' She stepped back from his desk and invited his scrutiny. Her thick golden hair was pulled back and tied with a blue ribbon, revealing two plain gold-hoop earrings. She was wearing a salmon pink shirt buttoned well up her chestbone, with a bra underneath; an ice-blue denim skirt which came at least halfway down her thighs; white bobbysocks; and soft-pink trainers. 'I look like an artless high school co-ed!'

The lawyer observed. And as he looked it occurred to Ella that perhaps her lawyer-guardian rather liked artless high school co-eds. She turned round slowly, with her hands on her hips, thrusting first her buttocks and then, as she came round again, her breasts, towards him. Yes, he definitely liked what he saw. She perceived a new strategy for getting her way with him, surprised that she had never thought of it before. She returned the head-to-toe scrutiny. It might even be fun.

'I can't have done anything too terribly bad,' she said as she came forward and perched on the corner of the desk beside him, swinging one leg and casually brushing it against his trousers. 'And you know it's only that I do like to oblige people whenever I can.' She smiled her very best.

He smiled back.

She didn't dislike him personally. Of course he must be

excited, she thought, by the sweet scent of life enjoyed which she exuded. And he never lectured her, never moralised. He just restrained. And goodness knows, her years in Manhattan had been plenty wild. It was only when she reached the gossip columns that he cut off her funds and reined her in.

'When I brought you back to Texas,' he said, 'I hoped you would find a strong, upstanding man. Someone with a firm enough hand to keep you under strict control.'

So that was his line, she thought with some amusement. She turned to face him more fully, swinging her foot between his legs and skimming his inside calf.

'But instead you took up a career. What on earth do you need a career for? And photography of all things!' He took a sheaf of colour prints from the top right-hand drawer of his desk and spread them on the surface beside her. 'Well it's got you in real trouble this time. You made the City Fathers' dinner-dance look like an orgy!'

'The rag asked me to take a few mug shots . . .'

'I don't know how you do it, Ella. Sex oozes out of everything you touch. If the sex isn't there to begin with, you conjure it up somehow. And then look how you use it!' He pointed to the worst examples: the subconscious inviting pose, the lewd sneer – the small change of erotic body language, isolated and exaggerated by her camera then reassembled and embellished by her darkroom technique to create a delicious, almost pornographic tableau of the cream of society.

'You've been very naughty, Ella.' He was working himself up. She could sense his pulse racing. 'A very naughty girl indeed.'

It was going like a script, she thought confidently.

'You're right. I've been naughty.' She hung her head coyly. Then she swung her leg once, slowly and deliberately, along his inner thigh until she pressed gently against the bulge in his trousers at the top. 'I've been very naughty. But you've got a big firm hand haven't you? I bet you could teach me a lesson.' She saw the lump in his crotch lurch bigger and decided to put all her cards on the table. 'I bet you could teach me a lesson on my bare bottom, and give me all the good advice you wanted with that big motivator between your legs, and then you could send me a long long way from here . . . all the way to New York . . . and you would never have to worry about me again.'

The lawyer scooped the prints together and put them away, his hands visibly shaking with excitement, and Ella, though feeling profoundly in control, thought it prudent to put down a limit marker.

'One spank for every naughty picture,' she said invitingly. There were ten of them.

She pulled her legs in, tucking her knees up under her chin, giving him the space in which to consider the deal she was proposing. Then she slowly and smoothly unfastened the bows on her trainers, slid a finger under the top loop of each lace and eased them loose, then on to the second and third loops, not giving him time to retreat, to cool. When the shoes were both loose she took them one at a time by the toe and heel and eased them slowly off her feet, letting them slip to the floor. The clean white cotton socks clung to the warm skin of her feet at first, compacted with the faintest fragrance of bodily exertion. She wriggled her toes lazily to free them.

'Behind the chair,' he said suddenly and with authority.

It had worked. Ella jumped off the desk with cheerful anticipation and took up position behind the big leather chair he had indicated. He remained seated but moved his chair out and to the side so that he could see her semifrontal, from head to toe.

'Up with the skirt.'

She smiled and started humming a teasing stripper's tune, wriggling her hips down while holding the skirt still with a flat hand on either side until her pink panties came into view.

'Cut the theatrics,' he said curtly.

She wiped the grin from her face at once. Okay, if that's the way he liked it, that's the way he'd get it. She matter-of-factly pulled the skirt up above her crotch and stuffed it into the waistband. It stuck out stiffly above her bottom like a dancer's tutu. The tight cotton briefs, their elastic containing the sweet briar of her pubic hair with neat efficiency, awaited orders.

'Off!' he said.

She casually hooked her index fingers inside the elastic waistband, pushed the panties down to her knees and stepped out of them, without a word.

He grunted, which she took as a sign of approval, and then he pressed a button on his telephone console, which she fervently hoped would not mean distraction.

The twin-set secretary entered, a severe but knowing smile on her face. Ella was affronted enough to show no embarrassment at all. That would be humiliating. But she was surprised. He had actually called in his secretary! What a nerve! But she allowed herself no visible reaction at all. It was one kick she wouldn't allow him.

'Her feet!' the lawyer ordered.

Ella stood bemused as the woman produced two strips of leather and dropped to her knees beside her. She swiftly tied one thong round Ella's right ankle, passing the other end round the leg of the chair and securing it with a hitch. She'd prepared all this, Ella thought; she'd even practised. Her resolve stiffened and she lifted her head with pride as she condescendingly opened her legs, allowing her left foot to be tied to the other corner. Then the secretary came and stood in front of the chair, facing Ella with a look of hungry contempt.

'Let's see the rest quickly,' the lawyer said, showing the first signs of impatience.

Ella stood aloof, passive, and the secretary went to work on the shirt buttons. But she was overexcited and couldn't manage her fingers. Careful not to appear insolent, Ella started to help her. She was feeling a certain rush to get on with it herself.

The loosened shirt slid from her shoulders to the floor. Then the grey little woman unfastened the bra from behind, and the skirt, and tossed them to one side so that Ella stood naked but for her white socks and the ties around her ankles. The man was silent. Ella looked at the ceiling and let him feast his eyes for a moment before taking the initiative herself by bending forward over the back of the big chair. She shivered with delight as her pubic hair brushed against the soft suede.

Now the secretary came round to the front, with two more leather strips which she tied around Ella's wrists. She pulled the wrists apart and down, tying one to the front right leg of the chair, the other to the left. Ella's crotch pressed harder against the chair back. Her labia, engorged with anticipation, were squashed against the smooth but resilient suede and she rocked briefly up and down on her toes to savour the contact. Her breasts, too, touched the seductive fabric. Her nipples were brushed into pinnacles of raw and urgent desire as they nestled on the seat of the chair. But they were hidden away from view now, one aspect of this payment of pleasure which would remain her delight alone.

Ella lifted her head from its position of rest on the front of the chair seat and watched as the lawyer opened the central drawer of his desk, took out a cane and handed it to his secretary. Then she lowered her head and concentrated on the centres of her energy, her breasts and her crotch, the one almost private and the other unusually exposed.

The first swish of the cane came like a tiny whisper, a tease on one cheek. And then its mate, on the other. Ella instinctively thrust out her bottom as far as she could with her wrists and ankles tied. The next stroke came a little harder, across both cheeks at once. There was a delectable pause, and again Ella thrust out her bottom to meet the cane. This time it made a smacking noise and smarted. Ella felt a tremendous rush of sexual energy coursing round the target she was presenting. She pictured her cheeks turning red, felt the rosy glow radiating outwards to her public and inwards to her crotch. And this time when she heard the swish coming she flinched from it imperceptibly, and felt the rush of the blow thrilling its way straight through to the core of her sex. Now her clitoris stretched out from her lower lips and kissed the suede as each stroke hit above, and from her upper lips came a rhythmic gasp of rapture and encouragement.

There was another noise, too; almost a panting. Ella

twisted her face sideways briefly and saw that the secretary had one of her hands up her own skirt. Ah! How she loved it! An actor delights in moving his audience to laughter or to tears, but Ella's art found its surest acclaim when its public couldn't keep its hands off its sex. She thrust out her bottom and the next stroke came harder, more agitated, with even heavier breathing. It was wonderful! She had brought the tight little secretary to this. Any moment and the third party would lose control of herself . . .

But what about the second party? Ella couldn't see. Then the lawyer stood. He came towards her, moving into her field of vision to let her see. But the cane kept coming down; there was a continuous smarting heat, pumping lust and desire throughout her body. He stood beside her face so she could see that he had his cock out of his trousers, and he, too, had his hand on his sex. It was a splendid big dick. She could smell its splendour. She wanted to feel it, taste it. She wanted it to pierce the passionate heat of her crotch and quench her fire. But he was in no hurry. She watched his hand slide slowly up and down the thick shaft, bearing the loose skin with it. The head was red and glistening, straining like a dog on a leash but still under the control of its master. And then the panting noise behind her lurched into a loud, chaotic crisis and the caning stopped.

'Now!' Ella begged, addressing the cock in front of her. 'Come in me now!'

He made no answer except to increase significantly the speed and rigour with which his hand slid up and down the length of his stiff cock.

'Come on!' she pleaded, pulling on the straps which tied her wrists and repeatedly thrusting her cunt against the chair-back in her frustration. 'Please! Please! I need the rest of my lesson!' And as she spoke these words the penny dropped. This was his lesson, not hers at all. She chaffed at her bonds and called out for his cock. 'Fuck me! Fuck me! Please!'

But with the cold detachment which for him was the hallmark of his profession he ignored her pleas and stuck stubbornly to his brief. She watched in silent rage as he suddenly let go of his cock and it rose commandingly under its own momentum and seemed to nod at her like a huge pointing finger . . . 'I'm warning you, I'm warning you' . . . as it bobbed up and down vigorously, and spat at her.

She slumped down in the enforced pose she now found humiliating beyond account. As lawyer and secretary tidied themselves Ella tried to contain the double heat of her arousal and her anger. She tried to dampen her feelings with cooling rational thought, like lawyers can't count for one thing. And lawyers have precious little regard for justice, or fairness, or keeping deals . . .

He crouched in front of her with a map of England and she watched with mounting despair as the pencil he was holding swept over London, passed beneath Stratford, moved over and beyond Bristol, and came to rest with great precision in a blank spot somewhere sort of in the middle.

'Home,' he said emphatically. 'Where you're going to be a very very good little girl indeed!'

Ten minutes later and fully dressed in the outer office, Ella kept repeating to herself like a mantra, 'Never again . . . never again . . . The likes of that will never happen to me again . . .' while her legal guardian's secretary spelled out the details of her banishment.

'A cottage has been rented in your name. And arrangements have been made for you to collect from the village post office just sufficient money each week to sustain a simple rural existence. All your other assets . . .' The woman paused to peer at Ella over the rim of her glasses. 'Financial assets, that is, and access to credit, have been frozen.'

'Whereas you've got a post-orgasmic flush right up the side of your face,' Ella said.

But there was no question of any blush to join it. 'You can take your camera,' the woman told her. 'Our paper is interested in a series of photo-essays on quaint English customs. That should be an interesting challenge for someone of your particular talents.'

One of the men Ella had sat next to on the bench in the lobby passed through for his interview. He had seemed powerless then, and she had pitied him. Now he put her in mind of big Texas, with its big skies, big ideas and big money. Maybe he was disputing the title to an oilfield, or the patent on a satellite system. She was heading for a tiny village in a smug little wood where the sky was always as low as a rain cloud, and she could dispute nothing.

'And there'll be someone to keep an eye on you,' the secretary said in conclusion. 'Someone in keeping with the place, naturally.'

Ella raised her eyebrows involuntarily.

'He writes a little nature-lover's diary for a provincial newspaper once a week, and draws birds.'

Now there's a challenge, Ella thought mischievously.

'His name is George Goode.'

And with George Goode, Ella determined, she would start to enjoy her revenge.

There was no harm in a little practice first, however. Ella chose the captain for her purpose and when he came aft to stretch his legs she asked if she could see his cockpit.

The company jet had been laid on presumably to ensure safe and prompt delivery of its cargo. Ella had felt rather flattered and spent the first part of the flight taking advantage of its creature comforts. She had a foot massage and manicure during cocktails, then a superb farewell to Texan cuisine with roast game hen in red chilli gravy, pine nut and scallion pilaf, and peppered zucchini. The white zinfandel was a little disappointing but the cognac more than made up for it. They put down at Newark to refuel and the Manhattan skyline, clearly visible across the river as they took off again, gave her a pang of regret. Then the light started to fade, the cabin staff stopped fussing about, and the captain came out to stretch his legs.

'Sure I'll show you,' he said. 'It would be my pleasure.'

'No, *my* pleasure,' she answered emphatically. 'But I'd like it even more if your accomplice here could go and polish the brass or something, so there was room for you to show me the ropes.'

The captain sent his co-pilot packing. Then he leaned forward and flicked a couple of switches. 'We're flying automatic,' he said, 'but someone has to keep an eye on things.'

'I'm used to having men's eyes on me, Captain, and I don't like competition. But under the circumstances . . .' She slid into the co-pilot's seat and peered out of the windscreen. 'Where are we?'

'We crossed the coast of Maine a few minutes ago.' He sat down in his own seat, next to her. 'Now we're fifteen hundred feet above the North Atlantic.'

Speed, altitude, danger; wind and waves; deepening dusk. These competitors she relished. And she knew she would get more than her share of his attention.

She asked, 'Can I touch your joystick?'

'Sure. It's not doing anything right now.'

Ella went straight for his cock, squeezing it masterfully through the fabric of his uniform. 'Yes and no,' she said, as she felt it stir and stiffen. Then in one deft movement she stood and turned to face him, swinging a leg over the mechanical joystick and lifting her skirt to show her pantieless crotch enveloping its shaft. She completed her entrapment with a long French kiss which she ended only when she was absolutely certain that she had him.

'Let me secure the door,' he stuttered, leaning past her to press a button.

Ella wrapped the top of her thighs tighter round the metal shaft of the joystick and rubbed her cunt up and down it. 'Fly me,' she said. 'Fly me manually while I undress.'

'But I can't see!' he pleaded.

'You'll see plenty in a minute,' Ella smiled as she started unbuttoning her blouse. When he flicked another switch and leaned forward to speak into the cabin mike she slapped a hand across his mouth and announced herself: 'No interruptions for a little while, please. The captain has kindly volunteered to give me a lesson in astral navigation.' She turned the mike off and told him again to fly manual.

Within a minute Ella was naked and the pilot's hands were on the joystick. As he pulled it towards him the shaft slid between her moist labia and she hugged the movement with her clitoris. The pole was slippery already from her juices. She felt the plane bank and rubbed herself deliciously as the stick came back against her. She was flying the thing with her cunt!

'I'll keep it steady,' she said. 'Get your cock out.'

The captain loosened his belt and, still sitting, slithered his trousers and underwear down to his ankles. Ella lurched when she saw his zealous cock and two enormous silken balls with their pale downy hair, squashed against the cushion of the seat. The captain grabbed at the controls, frantically switching back to automatic, and Ella laughed to herself at the bead of fluid which appeared unsummoned from the tiny hole at the tip of his penis. Struggling to control himself as well as the plane, she thought.

With the tip of her finger she smeared the dribble of translucent fluid over the glans of his penis, making it glisten all over. Then she leaned way back until her bare skin touched the instrument panel. She shivered with excitement as the cold glass of a dial pressed against her side and a row of sharp metal switches dug like teeth into her buttocks.

He had an eye on the plane's switches as well as her own. But she wasn't the least bit impatient or jealous. It was like an orgy. She let the instrument panel embrace her. There was a slippery rod at her cunt and an eager mouth at her bottom. She made love to both in her mind as she rolled her soft flesh between them, enjoying the man watching as his hands roamed. He reached for her breasts; buttons, nipples, switches. She pulled her bottom cheeks open with her hands. Altitude indicator and chronometer vied for the pleasure of rimming her. She slid her clitoris down the slippery scented stick . . .

And then she leaped from the joystick to the captain's face, pressing his head back against the headrest of the seat and searching for his tongue with her cunt. He plunged into her obligingly and she pinned him there, blind, while she fumbled for the switch which turned on the intercom through to the rest of the plane. He started groaning. It was a virtuoso mix of surprise, pleasure, lust and discomfort. He didn't know that everyone on the plane was listening. She encouraged him with sounds of her own. But she was having to stand on tiptoes with her legs astride. And she was soon ready for something more engaging. She felt for his cock. It was pointing straight up at her, big and stiff. She stroked it up and down, inspiring more savoury sounds for the entertainment of the crew next door. She cuddled those exquisite, enormous balls, squeezing gently and producing a rich soundscape of seduction. Then she slid the hub of her sex away from his face and down his chest. As she watched her progress downwards she saw how wet and ready she was. She smeared a trail of pungent lubricant across his wide lapels and black silk tie.

She loved uniforms.

The captain reached for her thighs and tried to pull her down on him quickly, so Ella leaned forward and smothered his face with her breasts. She wanted this at her own pace.

'Suck,' she said as she cupped her breasts together and forced both nipples into his mouth. And then again loud and clear over his muffled clamour, for the mike and her audience next door: 'Suck! Suck! Suck!'

Then she held his cock with one hand and slithered down to meet it. Holding her lips apart with her other hand, she kissed the tip of his glans with her clitoris and then sank in one greedy, slippery movement right around him, swallowing up every inch of cock until her clitoris kissed his pubic bone. She gripped him tight, clung to his bone, rasping on the huge throbbing organ stretching up inside her. And then from her hips she began the tiniest of movements, a rocking, a lifting and falling. But only by a fraction of an inch, because she wanted to feel full, she wanted the cock inside her. So she fucked him her way, bouncing her little trigger off the root of his cock until she was absolutely ready, a hairsbreadth from shooting.

She felt herself quieten, now she was primed. And she started sliding up and down to bring him alongside her. The higher she rose, the louder his sigh; the swifter she fell, the deeper his gasp. His cock was stationary. She was fucking it. Up and down, up and down. It was his mouth that was moving, and she listened to its accelerating rhythm along with the crew. She fucked and she listened until she knew that she had brought him up to the very brink with her. Then she lifted herself so that only the very tip of him was in her, and stopped.

'No' he shouted. 'Go on! Go on!' He tried to thrust up into her. 'Finish me! Please!'

Then she slid down and fucked for all she was worth. He gasped at her. She bounced and twisted and gripped. They panted and heaved. And within thirty seconds his cock shuddered and pumped inside her as her cunt quivered and convulsed around him.

She collapsed like a dead weight on his lap, switching off the mike as she did so.

When the captain finally released the lock and Ella stepped back, fully dressed and composed, into the passenger cabin, she was greeted by an admiring round of applause from the crew. She allowed herself just a suggestion of a bow. Then she signalled for silence with a finger on her lips, eager that her puppet captain be left to face his acclaim later, by himself.

'I wish he would teach *me* astral navigation,' the chief stewardess said.

'Venus was in the ascendant,' Ella commented nonchalantly. She reclined her seat as far as it would go and slept the rest of the Atlantic.

They landed at Gatwick to clear Customs and then took off again heading northwest for the provinces. Ella was feeling distinctly brighter about her prospects in the old country, though she declined the offer of an English breakfast. As the cabin crew downed their sausage, bacon and egg, she freshened up and changed into clothes with more of a continental touch. She put on a small scarlet suspender belt with narrow straps and just a touch of lace at the front, with black nylon stockings; a tight, undyed leather skirt and loose Greek top with embroidered shoulders; and her Latin shoes with low sharp heels. She wanted coffee and croissants and then her Mr Goode for breakfast.

Ella insisted that the captain put her down, rev his engines, and zoom away. She wanted to walk off the runway by herself, mysterious, exotic, powerful . . .

2

NOT QUITE CRICKET

Ella's landing was a stunning event, frustrated by the total absence of an audience. They called it an airfield, not an airport, at Pod Magna. And there was no passenger terminal, just a clubhouse for the ex-RAF types who struggled valiantly to keep the place viable. When, laden with suitcases, she opened the door, she was met by the smell of stale beer and cigarette smoke. There was an unkempt youth glued to a video game in a corner. And at a table in the centre, sat a dapper but not unattractive man in his late forties who was the very picture of a country diarist.

Ella made a beeline for the table and leaned across it, giving him ample view of her cleavage, to plant a vigorous greeting kiss on his forehead.

'Eleanor Deedes,' she said cheerfully.

'Hello,' he answered minimally.

She sat down beside him and wondered what it was about his cup of tea that commanded more attention than her body.

'Do we have to whisper?' she whispered. 'Is it about to have babies or something?'

'It's cold,' he said.

'Well, I've got just the thing.' She leaned over to pull her suitcase closer, letting her skirt ride well above her stocking tops in his full view. She pretended she couldn't unfasten it, so she had to stand and bend over. She fussed around, thrusting her bottom out at him, her skirt riding higher and higher. The vertical straps of her suspender belt pressed into her soft flesh and she kept at it until she could feel the hem of her skirt running tight across her cheeks in the other direction. He could see the underhang of her bottom now, the English peachiness of her, framed in scarlet and black, only inches away from him.

'Here it is,' she said at last, producing a miniature bottle of whiskey. 'I raided the locker on the plane.' She plonked the bottle next to his cold tea, and her hand on his upper thigh. 'Let's get warmed up a bit. I know I'm here to report on quaint English customs, but this iceberg reception business is one that needs bending a little to suit the circumstances, don't you agree?'

The youth at the machine turned round for the first time. 'The old English custom of trying to seduce your landlord needs adapting too. You'll get nowhere with Ted.'

The scuffed suede boots, moleskin trousers and baggy Aran sweater housed a man about her own age. His shock of dark hair was uncombed, he wore a three-day stubble, and his expression suggested a polite but maverick intelligence.

'Speak for yourself,' Ella said flatly.

'I speak for you too,' he insisted. 'I understand I'm to provide the words to go with your pictures.' He held out his hand for her to shake. 'George Goode.'

'Ms Deedes,' she said saucily, as she shook it.

A few minutes later, on the way to Pod Parva in her landlord's car, Ella asked her new chaperone to fulfil his obligation and provide her with some words.

'Richard de Pode was a rogue Norman who bedded every Saxon wench within fifty miles,' he said.

'That's a good start.'

'He had two dozen bastards and he called every one of them Richard. They all died fighting each other except for two. That's how we got our market town and neighbouring village: Big Dick and Little Dick.'

Ella decided she liked him. 'And I'm going to live in Little Dick?' she asked incredulously.

'You can always go shopping in Big Dick,' Goode answered.

'You'll find everything you need at the post office in Pod Parva,' the landlord interjected from behind the wheel. Ted ran the post office and village stores and had been talked into fetching his new tenant in his car with the promise of good customer relations.

'I either walk or push pedals,' Goode explained. 'The MG stays in the city.'

'So you're not a native Dicker either?'

He shook his head in confirmation as he opened a wooden gate in a low privet hedge and ushered Ella through to the end cottage in a terrace of four. 'I was born into Silly Money, with capitals, and while I appreciate the privileges and pleasures that entails, I suffer a surfeit of silliness every once in a while.'

'You mean you overdose on sex?'

He shrugged his shoulders. 'Wine, women, song . . .'

'So you come here to wank in the woods and listen to the birds . . .' Ella ducked to get through the front door of her new home and realised with a shock that he wouldn't follow her in.

'So I retreat here periodically. I live simply, at the other end of this terrace, by myself. I watch birds. I sketch what I see, and I make a few notes for the paper.'

'And what do the birds do?' Ella asked. 'Don't they mate, and sing? Isn't that what nature's all about?'

But Goode had had enough. 'Look,' he said emphatically. 'I don't know why you're here, or why I've been landed with you. I suppose your daddy knows my daddy, or my family's firm owes your family's firm or something . . . global village and all that . . . But I'm not going to let you spoil this place for me. I'll point you in the right direction for your blessed pictures, and I'll give you some words to go with them if you want, but I'm not going to let you spoil this place for me. The Pods are strangely asexual and that's why I'm here. I'm not going to play your games.'

Ella flirted with the idea of telling him how beautiful he looked when he was angry, but her sexual intuition told her to wait. She would store him up, and savour the prospect.

'Why don't you start with one of *our* games?' He was being friendly again. Perhaps she had looked too crestfallen. 'There's a cricket match on the village green tomorrow. I'll take you.' And with that he was gone.

Ella looked around. The ceilings were low, with exposed

beams, but both kitchen and sitting room were otherwise spacious. The furniture was simple, made of old dark wood. The walls were white and the generous windows let in plenty of light, despite the climbing roses on every outside surface. The place smelled delicious and she declared herself well satisfied. The contemporary Little Dickers may have something a bit dried up and asexual about them, but this old house at least was sexy. It didn't speak of retired bank managers or week-ending executives, but of hearty down-to-earth people who left their boots by the back door and came in with big appetites. Ella had no idea where in England she had been born, but she hoped it was somewhere like this – where there were plenty of big-breasted girls with names like Fanny or Molly, and generous, bawdy lads who made imprudent, fallible heroes. She imagined she was jet-lagged, by about two hundred years.

She climbed the narrow staircase and opened the double windows in the main bedroom at the front of the cottage. Then she collapsed on the big bed, lying spread-eagled on her back, her chest bathed in sunlight.

'Cricket,' she mouthed pleasantly, enjoying some old folk memories or inventing her own . . . like a tall, earnest man in white flannels rubbing a hard leather ball up and down his inner thigh and leaving a red stain. Subconsciously while she daydreamed, her hand moved down to her own inner thigh, and rubbed up and down on the soft bare skin between stocking tops and crotch. There would be another man with a bat, getting ready to play the ball. He would raise and lower his equipment in nervous anticipation. Everyone else would crouch, snarling, hands poised over their sex, ready to catch him out.

Both of Ella's hands moved down to her crotch. Yes, she thought, I'll play cricket . . .

She took off her skirt and blouse and slithered down the bed until her bottom was poised on the edge of the mattress. She spread her feet, which rested on the floor, as far apart as she could, so that her black-stockinged thighs, with her wide-open vulva at the centre, formed a horizontal line along the end of the bed. This was the crease. Waiting in the pavilion there must be eleven players. It was going to be the game of their lives.

Ella summoned the opening batsman with her thoughts. The first was a good straight bat, his long stiff cock steady and reliable. He stood at the crease and readied himself. Ella held her labia apart and imagined his tool driving its way home as she slid two fingers into her vagina. With her other hand she started wicket-keeping, circling and teasing her clitoris. Number two was watching. They came in pairs, she remembered. But hers was a sticky wicket from the opening ball. Straight-bat crumpled, leaving it even stickier, and second bat rushed in. The second cock was sloshing up and down her crease in the first cock's sperm and he shared the same fate, rushing to his climax, fumbling his best shot, and losing all control in his excitement. Ella kept playing with herself as she conjured up the next two.

These were the bold strikers who worked as a team. Play them as a team, then, Ella told herself. She stood with one leg round the front of the bed and the other leg round the side, and bent forward until her crotch kissed the knob on the top of the low bedpost. This was the knob of number three. His partner came at her from behind, and as she rolled her crotch over the shiny knob she licked her index finger and slid it down the slit between her cheeks, pressing against her bottom hole and then slowly prising her way in. Number four. Both dispatched in short order.

She liked the teamwork. She conjured up five, six, seven and eight together. She felt like a captain arranging her fielders. She lay one of them down on the bed, on his back, and knelt across his groin, taking his cock inside her vagina. Call him Silly-mid-on. Then she leaned forward and summoned another to kneel behind her and cover her rosehole. Silly-mid-off. Number seven was to kneel above the face of Silly-mid-on, facing Ella, so she could take his bat in her mouth and suck it. He must be Point. She relished laying out her field for action. She crouched on her knees, with her bottom thrust out, one hand playing with her clitoris and the other with her anus, as she formed her mouth into an exaggerated O and made love to that space with her tongue.

But what about number eight? Who was number eight? Gully, perhaps. And then another word came to the overworked captain. Googly. And with a flash of inspiration she knew how to deploy her man. He would play a googly in Point's gully! She ordered him round the back of Point and told him his bat needed a little extra oil rubbing in. As he approached his crease she could feel Point tense himself. Penetrated from behind, the man's pucker was up. His bat flailed in her mouth and seemed doubly engorged, as though she were taking both of them in tandem.

Now all four were in play and Ella concentrated her attention. Good cricket was about timing. She moved her mouth smoothly, pressed gently with the fingers of her right hand, and worked her left hand quicker, and deeper, to bring all four of her players to a perfect pitch. And then they were there, and time momentarily stood still. Time for her to hear the birdsong, and feel the sun warm on her skin. The atmosphere was dense with heavy scents, from distant hedgerows to closer roses, lavender in someone's garden, and the deep musk of aroused, expectant bodies. Then wham! They all struck out at once! Hit for six! Wham! A four behind! Wham! Wham! A six at point! A six at deep point!

Ella rolled on to her back, her legs bent at the knees, and with the fingers of one hand deep inside her vagina and of the other fervently racing her clitoris to its climax she arched her back in supreme effort. Caught! She thrust her hot cunt up off the bed as she worked it. Run out! With her calves flexed and her thighs taut, her body arched along its whole length so she stood up from the bed on her heels and the back of her head . . . Stumped! Stumped! Stumped! And her bails went flying as a tortured, triumphant cry of 'Owzat!' echoed over the silent streets of Pod Parva.

The real game was choreographed at a rather slower and less sensual pace. And much to Ella's disappointment, Goode refused to watch it with her.

'Sorry,' he said with a disarming smile. 'But I'm way behind on my nesting survey.'

'Can't you survey the village birds today, and include me in?'

Goode shook his head, still smiling amicably. 'The patch I cover is three miles away, or I wouldn't have enough data. I told you the village had a sort of asexual aura to it. Even the birds don't seem to get into it here. You see a few collared doves in the conifers behind the church . . . the odd hedge sparrow and chaffinch . . . but they always seem to nest late and they only lay one clutch . . .' He hesitated as he sensed himself getting too serious. 'But you're not interested in birds.'

'I'm interested in the birds and the bees,' Ella said. 'Let's meet after the game and compare notes.'

Goode latched the little gate behind them and steered his ward along The Row towards the stretch of rough-mown meadow which was the village green.

'But first,' she said. 'Tell me about cricket for our feature.' She had left the Hasselblad at the cottage, and wore her old Minolta like the main item of her wardrobe, its black straps passing between breasts notionally restrained in a bikini top, and its leather case kissing the flesh of her midriff above a pair of scanty shorts.

'What do you want to know? I've done my homework.'

'Not all those silly words like googly and point. And not the rules, either. I'll find my own way through that lot. Tell me something about the sex of the game.'

'Well, it used to be male and female,' Goode answered, adopting the tone of lecturer, 'the original three stumps being the legs of a milkmaid's stool. Young men and women played it in the churchyards on Sunday afternoons, before churchyards became graveyards and the Puritans banned fun from the only day off work.'

'Hurray for them. But what happened to the women?'

'At the club where the modern game started they always drank a toast "To the immortal memory of Madge".'

'Madge the milkmaid?'

Goode waited while they passed an elderly lady walking in the opposite direction, then said: 'Madge was an eighteenth-century word for female genitalia.'

Ella was very impressed. She took his arm, like a madge

on the make in refined old England, and wouldn't let him retrieve it. 'If you act playboy as well as you act rural professor, I hope I bump into you in the big city sometime.'

They turned a corner on to a wider lane and the open space on which the game was to be played lay before them. 'The Little Dickers take the King's Arms,' Goode said, nodding towards the higgledy-piggledy timber-framed pub with a scratty, grey thatched roof, on their left. 'And the Big Dickers have the tea room.' Beyond the pub was a smart Georgian house beset with wrought-iron garden furniture. 'You'll find all sorts of men in there,' Goode said, with an air of handing her over.

She listed a few of her preferences: 'Studs, bulls, hound dogs, sports models . . .'

'I meant all social classes. Somebody once said, if the French nobility had played cricket with their tenants like the English, there wouldn't have been a revolution.'

That was quite enough of the wordsmith for Ella and she left him for the King's Arms in pursuit of some cricketing princes and paupers.

But she didn't find them. The team from the tea house trooped out to field and the other lot carried chairs out of the pub and sat along the side of the road to watch. They drank beer in half pints and talked about the mileage they were getting out of their cars, and what they'd seen on television the night before. There were a few women in attendance, and they talked about potting-on cuttings, or knitted. What happened on the pitch was even duller. Men stood as if they'd been planted. The bowling was infinitely slow, the batting drab and mechanical. All that changed was the monotony, which lengthened. Ella didn't even take a light-meter reading.

She tried flirting with the captain first, and failed dismally. She worked right down the batting order, and even on from there to some of the women. But she got nowhere. The harder she tried, the more energy she generated, the more turned-on she became herself. And so the more frustrated. But she was damned if she would masturbate again.

She tried focusing her energy on inanimate objects, to channel her libido into her art and take a few sensual pictures at least. She asked the men about their bats. They used words like weight, drive, and sweetness; willow, cane and linseed oil. Words with rich associations. But they made them sound dead. The balls were made of layers of cork quilting, bound with worsted; enclosed in white leather set with deer suet, with a hand-stitched seam. Ella was almost salivating at the earthiness of it. But through her lens they looked like hard red lumps.

When the first batsman was caught out, Ella tried the direct approach again. She thought he might be more relaxed now the pressure of the game was off. She followed him into the bar and introduced herself with a little congratulatory peck on the cheek, making sure he also felt her breasts brush against him. But he was drained beyond all hope and she soon gave up.

Re-emerging from the pub she noticed a bare arm protruding from the upstairs window of the tea room next door. It was executing a precise and unusual operation which she soon identified as scorekeeping. Several hooks had been screwed into the window ledge on the outside of the building and from these hung digits on large metal plates which were removed and replaced whenever runs were scored or wickets taken. Ella's strong exhibitionist streak grasped the possibilities at once. It could be her arm up there, with every eye turning periodically to endure or gloat over its handiwork, while inches below their line of sight, as she leaned forward, the scorekeeper was thrusting his cock in her from behind. She slipped into the building unnoticed and made her way swiftly upstairs.

He didn't notice her come in. He was watching the game intently through his wire-framed shades. An adolescent, late teens . . . and a late developer judging from his thin shoulders. But thin wiry cocks could be full of surprises. She knew him at once to be courteous as well as gawky, imaginative as well as inexperienced. His attention came back into the room as he made pencil dots to denote the over in a little scorebook in front of him, and he heard the squeak of her trainers on the wooden floor.

'Sorry, miss. Nobody is allowed in here during play.'

I'm not nobody, she wanted to say. I'm the sexiest

woman you've ever laid eyes on and I want to fuck. But she didn't want to scare him.

'I'm an investigative photo-journalist. There can be no secrets from me.' She took a few pictures. He refused to be distracted, though he politely obliged her when the poses she asked for didn't affect his functioning as scorekeeper. She leaned out of the window to let him feast his eyes on her legs and bottom. Then she complained about how hot it was and pulled her top well away from her breasts, making sure he saw as she bent forward and blew cool air over her stiff hot nipples. But there was not a hint of a rise out of him. He was gazing off into the distance again.

'You can score with me,' she said as she put her hand on his thigh and slipped it into his crotch, searching for the elusive lump. But he slapped her hand away without even taking his eyes off the distant umpire.

Ella was hopping mad. She wanted to teach him some real manners, there and then. But in a moment of blind panic she wondered if she was somehow to blame. She ran her hands down her sides and nearly burned herself with desire. Her energy, her appeal, her sexual aura was as strong as ever. But that expression, sexual aura, stopped her short. Goode had used it. He said the village hadn't got one. Could there really be something to it? Maybe the water supply was polluted. Or the building materials were radioactive. Or there was something in the air. Even the birds didn't have good sex, Goode said. She became acutely paranoid. Had her devious guardian sent her here on purpose to cure her, knowing what she would find? Or even worse, done whatever it was that had been done here on purpose, specially for her?

She fled the score-room shocked, appalled, uncertain, confused. There was one way to prove Goode wrong, and that was with the hard evidence of film. She had to get out there on the pitch and join in, the way she always did when she wanted art from her camera. She had to use all the energy available to her, all her skill and experience and animal power, and she had to take pictures with life in them. Real, throbbing, vital life.

'I want to go out on the pitch,' she told the captain.

He shook his head dogmatically. 'Players only.'

'What about those old dodderers?' she said, pointing to two pensioners in long white coats who were hobbling to some appointed place with the help of walking sticks.

'They're the umpires.'

'Then let me guest umpire! Give me a whistle and you'll never see fairer play!'

The captain laughed. But Ted the Village Stores leaned over from two chairs away and whispered: 'She could umpire square leg after we retire.' And Ella was so busy trying to wrestle meaning out of that, she didn't hear him add: 'She might be less trouble out there than in the tea room with the Magnas.'

For the rest of their innings, Ted calmly coached Ella in the single skill of observing a run-out from square leg, trying all the while to instil a sober sense of responsibility to the sport. When the Parvas took to the field half an hour later, the senior umpire, who was breathing heavily, gladly took the chance to wet his whistle and passed his white coat on to Ella.

The coat came down to her knees. It was stiffly starched white linen, with four buttons up the front, and before she walked on to the pitch she had managed to unhook her top and step out of her shorts. She was naked except for trainers, ankle socks and the umpire's coat.

She felt deliciously welcome at square leg, and sensed a tremendous change in the men as soon as they walked out with her. They were obviously aware of her in a way that none of them had been before, and it made a remarkable difference. They bore themselves with a certain anticipation, walked with a little swagger, moved their limbs like it was all a warm-up for something much much bigger. By the end of the first over they were strutting to their new positions like peacocks.

Ella was amazed at the speed of the change and was determined not to let it loose direction. She had to move too, from the crease by the road to the crease at the copse end, with her back to the spectators the whole way. She unfastened her top two buttons and took several pictures as she walked, to exercise her breasts and make sure they were well exposed.

She buttoned up as she turned in her new position. Now the game came alive! Muscles flexed like springtime, the air was electrified with lust. The ball hurtled through it with hope, vision, subterfuge . . . and was played with instinct and daring. She shot her film with a superb eye for the passion in it all. There wasn't one of them on the pitch who didn't want to make love with her now, who wasn't already making love to her.

Then she had a truly valiant idea: to consummate this love affair right here on the village green, in the middle of the game! To copulate with cricket!

As she passed the captain at the end of the over she said she needed to put some new film in. Could the men make a circle round her, to cut down the light? Could one of them help her?

After the next over.

She heard the news going round. She felt the buzz. With her back to the road again, she undid all the buttons. She put her hands in her pockets and held her coat open. Soft pink trainers and white ankle socks. Smooth long limbs, supple but with enough flesh to shout 'eat me!' A burning bush of auburn hair, pouting from the pelvis beneath a silken-smooth abdomen. Deep rolling curves from hips to waist to bosom, the landscape of Venus. Breasts at once pendulous and pert, all things to all men. Magical wonderful pending sex. Her face clear, beautiful, inviting.

She waited like a goddess in the wings while the balls whizzed and the bats struck. Then the over was over, and she walked quickly to the crease.

'It won't take a minute,' she said, as the men gathered round.

'Who do you want?' the captain asked.

At this point a little selfishness was permissible, she felt. She pointed to a Saxon hulk of a man with a look of Wild Edric to him. Then she went down on her hands and knees.

The rest of the team made a tight circle standing shoulder to shoulder, their baggy flannel trousers making an effective curtain round Ella and her Saxon.

'Something to do with her camera,' a woman in the crowd surmised, without stimulating much interest.

Ella lifted the coat up to her waist and opened herself to the Saxon. But the thought of his rude, greedy organ coming inside her sight unseen was too much for her. She rolled over and lay on her back on the grass, the coat now huddled round her shoulders, her knees bent up to her waist and wide apart. And with a shock of surprise turning swiftly into a smile of happy indulgence she discovered that her human shield was facing inwards, not outwards as she had expected.

Half of the men had their cocks out of their flies already. Her smile broadened. The others soon caught up. Eleven big dicks of the Little Dickers. She saw enough of the Saxon's before it went inside her to confirm that she had chosen well. But she didn't try to match dicks to faces. She just concentrated on dicks . . . ten of them leaning over her, gorging themselves on her . . . bobbing up and down, their bright red heads retreating down their shafts then darting out again like subterranean animals. There were young brazen dicks, older dicks, dicks with thick veins coursing up their length.

The man kneeling at her open crotch came inside her. It was all happening so quickly! Then she saw the first of those above her shudder and bob with a sudden urgency and intensity . . . and shoot a thin stream of clear fluid across the circle. She felt a warm splat on her thigh. Another cock creased up and the hand that stroked it milked a thick white cream from the little hole at the tip. A third cock pulsed violently and shot a viscous gob of sperm onto the Saxon's flank. Ella watched them all, smelled them, felt them. She was having sex with eleven gorgeous cocks. She soaked up their sperm like spring rain. And then as though filled by all the team at once she joined them in almighty orgasm . . . united, fuelled, empowered . . . and refreshed . . .

'It was bizarre,' Ella told Goode when he rejoined her in the early evening. 'For hours I couldn't get a rise out of any of them, no matter how hard I tried. It was like a sexual vacuum. Then I went out on the pitch and it was like a sexual vortex. They were all over me, all of them.'

The birdwatcher frowned. 'How peculiar.'

'Well,' Ella deferred. She'd never had it quite that way before but she wouldn't want him to underrate her imagination.

'Oh, no offence,' he said distractedly. 'I mean my birds, too. I found a grasshopper warbler right here on the green!'

'That's peculiar?' she said sarcastically.

'It's not a particularly rare bird, but it's incredibly secretive. It nests in thick cover and you very rarely see it, just hear it. We don't even know for sure where it winters, it's so private. And yet here was a female and a whole clutch of males, hanging up their sign on the village green like a travelling circus.'

Ella was a pleasure seeker, in her view a guiltless natural channel for the wonderful sexual energy of her species. But the channel had been blocked. And then it had opened like a floodgate.

'Something very funny is going on,' she said enticingly. 'And I'm going to get to the bottom of it.'

3

ALL WELL AND GOOD

Ella slept soundly in her new home. She was woken by a long sequence of reverberating dongs from the church clock and she struggled to the windows in her black satin camisole to close them. An hour later the clock sounded again with an even longer fanfare, as if to congratulate her on putting together an excellent brunch for herself and shedding the slinky camisole at last for a cotton sun-dress with a bold floral print and thin shoulder straps.

Goode knocked courteously at the open kitchen door and stuck his head in.

'Watch that pickle!' he warned cheerfully. 'They say the devil never comes near Pod Parva for fear of being chopped up and put in Mrs Pringle's pickle.'

Ella deliberately scooped the last of the spicy, piquant pickle on to a finger of bread and slid it enticingly between her hungry, pouting lips.

It was enough to stall any impulse Goode may have felt to step inside. He fidgeted in the doorway while she completed her performance and then said hurriedly: 'The well-dressing committee starts work this afternoon in the village hall. Lots of colour and tradition: a good photo opportunity as they say. And it runs all week. I'll let you have the words once you're hooked.' And with a half-wave of his camouflaged bird-survey board he was gone.

As radiant as a bird of paradise in her colourful dress, Ella dragged her chair over to the open doorway and perched in the full sun while she finished her meal. An enormous spray of rambling rose drooped below the lintel of the door, the feminine fragrance of its coppery pink flowers a luxury of reassurance and excitement. She lingered over her first glass of the local tipple, reflecting that if Mrs Pringle packed the devil's flesh into her pickle, she surely kept a little of his spirit for her perry. Then she reached for her Roman sandals, slipping her nicely tanned feet into the white leather and leisurely criss-crossing the thongs round her ankles and calves before tying them just below the knee. She stood for a long enriching draught of scent before stepping through the arch and sauntering forth in search of the village hall.

There she found a small group of mostly elderly people with an air of sombre purpose as if they had gathered to debate the choice of next Sunday's hymns. One of them tried to shoo her away: 'The erection ceremony isn't for three days.'

'Maybe I can help you get it up a little quicker,' Ella answered glibly.

A stony-faced woman tried to bar the entrance with her formidable frame, but the expert at inspiring quick erections slid past. She shot a few pictures and as though now in possession of incriminating evidence, knew that she would not be expelled.

Precisely what the evidence amounted to, Ella wasn't sure. It didn't look very exciting. The men were fiddling about with carpentry tools and bits of wood. Wood could be extremely erotic. Ella loved to slide her hand along a piece of newly planed and sanded pine. But these men were hammering grey planks together with no grace or sensibility, arguing about which piece went where. The women, all in plastic aprons, were clustered round a long table. They were each kneading a lump of something on a flat board. Bread-making was extremely sexy. All that pummelling and pounding on warm rising dough, while the germ within was making babies by the million. But these women were poking at it nervously, as though it might bite them. They seemed frightened of getting dirty.

'She was taking pictures at the cricket,' one of the women said.

'I'm researching English customs. For an American paper.'

'More Americans,' the woman grumbled, making room

for Ella to nudge in the circle. 'It's useless trying to keep them out.'

It was clay they were working, Ella saw, but they were kneading it like dough. And opposite her, she noticed at once, there was a younger woman, about her own age. She had a beautiful face, strikingly clear and very soft, almost too soft, with a touch of sadness. Ella fought back an impulse to reach over and stroke it.

'We puddle the clay the men have dug,' the woman on Ella's right explained. 'And then tomorrow we'll smooth it into the frame they're making, about an inch deep, and start mapping out the design. The day after that we'll start petalling, and you can come and work with us.'

But Ella was working with them already. She was shooting film, trying to capture the earthiness of the scene, working round to the other side of the table. Someone spoke to the younger woman, calling her Susan. Ella felt herself weaken momentarily at the knees.

Susan.

She could see her from behind now.

Susan was wearing tight blue jeans, size eight at the most, tucked into little white pixie boots. Here was a genuine English village maiden, soft and shy, and Ella wanted to touch more than her face. She wanted to run her hand down the perfect arch of her back and over that sweet petite bottom, and then up underneath her prim striped blouse to cup those cute tiny breasts and frisk their pretty nipples. She worked with her camera. But she didn't want to screw Susan through the lens, the way so many male cameramen worked. She wanted to search out the sexuality, draw on it, colour it and celebrate it.

Susan was not co-operating, however. She seemed oblivious of the effect she was having on Ella. She seemed to inhabit her body like a schoolgirl might a Wendy house. She poked at the clay prudishly, just like the others.

When the frame was finished, the men left. One of the women filled a metal pail from a tap in the corner and walked round flicking water to wet the wood all over. Then she dragged out an old tin bath tub and they all in turn carefully lowered in their lumps of clay. Susan dribbled water on top to keep it moist overnight while the others cleaned up and Ella feigned a problem with her camera to keep her posing. She asked her if she would mind standing just so, as an excuse to put a hand on her hip and guide her into position. It was a deliciously tender body and this first slight contact made her hungry for more.

The other women were leaving.

'Do you call that puddled?' Ella asked Susan, in a desperate ploy to hang on to her.

Susan looked at the clay, not the questioner. She had medium-length black hair parted down the middle, and two thick swathes of it fell across her narrow face when she looked down. 'Not really,' she answered meekly. 'We'll have another go at it tomorrow, I suppose.'

'You and I could have it done in half an hour, if we did it properly.'

Susan made no response except to flick her hair out of her eyes and stare in astonishment as Ella unfastened her sandals and stepped out of them and then pulled up the skirt of her frock and tucked it in the elastic of her knickers. They were the only two left and Ella grabbed Susan's arm for support as she stepped onto the slippery clay inside the tub.

'This is the way to puddle clay where I come from.'

Susan tried to pull her arm away but Ella kept a firm hold of it as she worked her feet up and down and flattened the individual lumps into one squelchy mass.

'What did she mean, about *more* Americans?' Ella asked. 'You get a lot of tourists?'

'Oh no,' Susan answered, with a false tone of relief which to the more experienced woman shrieked of a desperate need for a fling with a colourful stranger. 'We don't get any tourists here. She meant the Americans who bought Pod Manor.'

'And who are they?'

'I've never seen them. I don't really know.'

No, she wouldn't, Ella thought. And soon she would be rushing home to help Mummy with the tea. But what a gorgeously tender, untrammelled body!

'I ought to be going,' Susan said.

'But I need you!' Ella insisted. 'And look how well it's coming along.' Together they looked at the thick globules of red clay oozing up between Ella's toes. 'I need some more water . . .'

Susan reached for the pail and flicked water on to Ella's feet, and then moistened the entire surface of clay. Now she was an accomplice. And she could obviously appreciate the effectiveness of the method.

'Why don't you join me?'

Susan shook her lovely slinky hair in the negative and said she had to go soon to help with tea.

'We could have it done in ten minutes, if you joined me.' Ella sensed that an appeal to daring, or mischief, would be counter-productive, but simple efficiency might do the trick, and she was right. Susan silently lifted one foot and slid the pixie boot off by the heel, revealing a delicate white naked foot. Then the other one. Erotic shivers tickled Ella's crotch. Then Susan pulled up the legs of her jeans as far as they would go, which was only to mid-calf.

'You could take them off,' Ella suggested as nonchalantly as possible. But Susan had already stepped into the tub, flexing her fragile tendons and arching her foot into a heavenly curve of nervous expectation as her toes came down on the cold wet clay, and she pretended not to hear.

They squelched together. Ella felt she was having sex already. The raw earth working its way up between her toes and around her ankles . . . her long legs glorying in their nakedness . . . and the angelic physical presence beside her . . . all conspired to bring her to a delicious pitch of sexual alertness. She was enjoying herself and felt no need to rush towards orgasm. And she knew now instinctively that Susan was a virgin. The woman was her own age, with a tremendous capacity to give and enjoy sexual pleasure, but she was not as yet thoroughly inhabiting her body. Perhaps it was simply inexperience, or ignorance. Or maybe she was hung up in some adolescent mind-frame. She had an air of someone with a little knot somewhere from the past, waiting to be exorcised. Ella launched blindly into an impoverished schoolgirl fantasy, playing for time and hoping for a lead.

'This reminds me of once at school when the biology teacher took us pond-dipping. He was a real tartar, the sort of biologist who's all books and microscopes and never gets his hands dirty. When he wanted some fresh material for making slides he made us girls take off our socks and shoes and tuck our skirts in our knickers, just like this, and wade into the pond to get it. The edge was bare clay and when I'd collected my algae I'd squelch around in it just for fun. I wasn't the mischievous kind at all; in fact I was a bit of a teacher's pet.'

Ella smiled to herself and deliberately brushed her knee against the thigh of the real teacher's pet beside her.

'I was mortified once when he called us in and I slipped in my puddle and landed fair and square on my backside. My knickers clung to my cheeks with brown wet mud. No way would he have me back in his classroom! He told me to stand exactly where I was, with my hands on my head, until he came back and told me to move. And so I did.'

She demonstrated with her hands clasped together on top of her head, her legs apart, her bosom thrusting at the bewildered Susan.

'And then he forgot all about me. It seemed like hours. My arms went stiff and my knickers dried out, stuck to my skin. But worst of all, I needed to pee. I needed to pee so badly I couldn't move a muscle, not even if he came and told me I could go. It was agony standing still: it would be *impossible* to move. I couldn't imagine a way out. I wanted to die.

'Then the art mistress came by, on her way home after classes. She was my favourite teacher; gentle and understanding. But that made it worse! It was too utterly humiliating! And still I couldn't move!' Ella picked up the bucket and sprinkled more water around her feet. ' "What on earth are you doing?" she asked me, shocked. So I told her. Then her eyes melted with pity and she made as if to put an arm round me. But I flinched away. And that nearly made me burst!

' "Don't!" I begged her. "It hurts!"

' "Where?" she asked.

'Something in my eyes must have told her. She put her

hand out and touched me very gently, right there.' Ella reached forward and placed the flat of her hand against Susan's jeans over her crotch. 'And she smiled understandingly as my pee seeped out against all my efforts at control and soaked my knickers and dribbled and then poured hot and endless over her loving fingers and down my thighs to splash on my feet in the clay.'

Ella had wanted to splash water over Susan's crotch, to bring wet and dirt together with sex to mimic the release and the sense of freedom, but Susan took the bucket from her and stepped away.

'I was crying by then, pee still pouring out of me unstoppably, and I started shaking with what I thought ought to be shame but was really relief . . . heavenly, wonderful, pleasurable relief.'

Susan washed her feet in the bucket and patted them dry on a towel. 'What happened then?'

'The teacher took me to her apartment,' Ella answered, much encouraged. 'She stripped me and put me in the shower. Then she undressed and came in with me. It was just what I needed. I felt so helpless. She lathered my entire body. She cleaned the caked-on mud from my bottom. She soaped her hands and slid them between my legs. Then she rinsed me clean. I think she even kissed away my tears. She wrapped me in a huge bath towel and cuddled me. Me, in tenth grade, cuddling with my teacher! I think I'd always had a crush on her. It was blissful.'

Susan pulled on her boots. 'I think we're all done now,' she said matter-of-factly, looking at the smooth sloppy clay.

Ella smiled from the frontiers of her fantasy, knowing very well that she and Susan were far from being all done now.

When Goode next put his head round her kitchen door, Ella asked him what this well-dressing was all about.

'Pacifying the water gods,' he said.

'How appropriate.'

'A pagan business but harmless enough.'

'I couldn't agree more.'

He found her passive smile disconcerting. 'They stick

flower petals in clay to make a picture,' he added. 'And put it up near where the pond used to be, to appease old Neptune.'

'I think it's a lovely idea. I'm going to help.'

'They make pictures of birds and trees and so on,' Goode said, as he walked with her along The Row. 'Nothing very cosmopolitan.

She turned on him with delight. 'Not even a mermaid?'

Susan was wearing purple jogging pants and a baggy sweatshirt for the next stage of the operation. Ella found them very fetching. The clay had been trowelled into the ten-foot square frame and smoothed flat, and sheets of tracing paper with the design drawn on them laid on top. Two older women worked at the foot and Susan at the top, pricking through the paper into the clay with a cocktail stick to mark the outline of the picture.

'You like sports?' Ella asked as she sat next to Susan and started pricking.

Susan shook her head.

'Jogging? Aerobics?'

More shakes. The shiny black hair fell forward and Ella wanted to kiss the soft spot at the back of her neck.

'Ever had a massage . . . you know, in the gym?'

A single, very definite shake. Ella decided that if she was going to carry the entire conversation she might as well do it her way.

'I had my first massage a long time ago . . . the day after the shower I was telling you about, with my art teacher. I went back to her place the next day to say thank you and she asked me if my arms were still feeling sore. They weren't really, but I had a feeling she wanted me to say yes. So she stood behind me and started to rub my shoulders. It was lovely. She worked down each arm in turn, gently squeezing, stretching and then stroking me smooth. It was wonderful. I didn't want it to stop. I said the trouble with biology classes was that you didn't learn anything about human bodies; not anything useful anyway. So she asked me if I'd like a massage all over, to learn something lovely about the human body.'

Susan edged away towards the top corner. If she really wanted to avoid what was coming, Ella thought, she should have moved towards the two women who were nattering to each other down the other end, not further from them.

'She told me to strip off and lie face down, and then she undressed too, so we should be equal, she said, and more equally in touch. Then she started on the soles of my feet and gradually worked up my calves, the backs of my knees, my thighs, buttocks, back . . . with plenty of oil in her warm hands . . . cobbling, hacking, kneading and then draining away. Ah! You know what it's like, the luxury of total caress!' It was a rhetorical question. Susan was pricking away with her methodical efficiency.

'But when I turned over on to my back and she reached my genitals it was something else! "We have special techniques for this area," she said. She pushed my thighs apart and knelt between them. And then she took hold of a single pubic hair, in the top corner of the triangle, and pulled on it slowly and gently, and then let go. She searched out the next between her thumb and forefinger and pulled again, long and slow. She worked her way right along, pulling every hair it seemed to me. And then back again lower down, pulling every hair right down to the bottom tip of my bush. It was an ecstatic tease, almost a torture . . . not because she pulled too hard, but because of the tantalising attention to detail. Pricking out these holes brought it all back to me. It was like a thousand little pin pricks in reverse, building up into something really special.'

The something special had to wait. The tissue paper was lifted off, now the outline was pricked into the clay, and they had to go over it with black hemlock seeds. Ella kept the story of her genital massage going in parallel.

'Then she traced the lines of my flesh with a single finger dripping with oil . . . down the crease between my abdomen and thigh, right from the hip down the sides of my bush, along the edge of my vulva to my anus. Then back up the other side. Again and again, infinitely slowly. Then gradually she focused in on the vulva, circling the outer lips, around the top of my clitoris, never touching it, down to my bottom . . . round and round . . .'

The more she stretched out the movement, keeping her voice slow and sensuous, the more Ella was drawn into her fantasy herself. She nudged closer to Susan than ever, not with much hope of a physical breakthrough with her, but desperate to rub her crotch against a table leg as she reached forward with her seeds.

And then it was lunchtime.

After lunch came the petalling. A second squad of worthy ladies had been scouring the meadows and hedgerows, gathering flowers. Now they started filling in the spaces between the lines of seeds by pressing individual petals into the clay. Susan was plucking tiny pieces off the head of a yellow marigold, and pressing them into the round space in the sky which was to be the sun.

'It's a bit painting-by-numbers isn't it?' Ella said. 'My art teacher would never have approved. She'd have encouraged some spontaneous, individual creativity.' She picked a red rose from a tray and held it next to Susan's sun. Then she bent down and ran her nose around the edge of it, spiralling inwards to the conical, unwrapped centre and breathing deeply with delight.

'That's what my art teacher did to me next.' Ella whispered. 'First with the tip of her nose and then with the tip of her tongue. My love's like a red, red rose . . . Round my outer lips, and then the inner, swollen and red by now just like this rose. Then on to my bud, the heart of my display, tingling with the raw freshness and joy of it all.'

Susan plodded on with her work, pulling off petals and jabbing them in the clay.

'And when my teacher sucked at my bud, I felt my nectar rushing out of me. She plunged her tongue deep inside me and swept it round, lapping up my juices. My rosebud quivered, my petals trembled; stem, branch, root . . . the whole plant of me shook like fury, as though a storm had come up out of nowhere.'

All this poetry was making Ella's knickers soggy, but was having no effect at all on Susan.

'And I've been coming happily ever after,' Ella said forlornly to end her story. She reached for the tray of roses.

'Just look at all these different cunts,' she said loud

enough for all to hear but quickly enough for none but Susan to be sure. 'Some saying, "Aren't I lovely, come and pick me." Some spread open fit to pleasure the whole world. Some too puffed up with self-importance and some too tight for their own good.'

She took a few pictures but she knew there was no vital presence to them. Then she tried a bit of petalling herself, filling in the sky with blue hydrangea. Susan soon corrected her.

'You must overlap them properly, like roofing tiles,' she said. 'So they throw off the water if it rains.'

Not like roofing tiles, Ella thought to herself. Like chain mail, my little English maiden with your stiff upper lip and your stiff lower lips, locked inside your suit of armour.

On her way home she stopped at the other end of The Row, three doors from her own, where Goode lived. She was feeling a little sorry for herself. I need some good sex, she thought. But she didn't say so to Goode. How could she beg sex from a man who barred the way into his home with his arm and asked her with a smile on the doorstep if she'd had a colourful day?

'What's this I hear about Americans in the village?' She needed a rest from tradition. She needed some current practice.

'You know I don't come here to socialise,' Goode answered. 'But from what I gather they're old, fat and reclusive. If you want to go visiting you'll find them two miles out towards Pod Magna, in a pretentious mock-Gothic castle called Pod Manor. You'll recognise it by the surrounding tall pines and dense laurels, and the brick wall with barbed wire on top.'

That night Ella dreamed of Susan in her chain mail. She was transformed into a Joan of Arc figure, small and soft in her suit of armour. She imagined her naked inside the metal. Her white delicate-boned feet were hot and sweaty inside their rigid casing with long pointed toes. The nipples on her tiny breasts brushed erect against her breastplate.

And her virgin labia rubbed as she walked against the hard crotch of her corselet.

Then she turned into a mermaid, with no crotch at all. Just silver scales from the tip of her tail to her abdomen. But what enchanting breasts!

When Ella woke she determined she would get her revenge. The well-dressing was erected late that evening. She would steal out in the night and bring the boring landscape to life.

She spent the morning scouring village gardens in search of silvery leaves and petals, and stealing them. She made sketches. And she practised petalling until she could perfect the seductive mermaid and the erotic knight errant.

After supper Ella went out with her camera round her neck and her shoulder bag full of petals. From the front of the pub she watched the committee trying to get their tableau vertical on the green without all the clay falling out. She took a few shots but the only life was in the sky. There the water gods, in the form of puffed-up rain clouds, struggled against the dying sun which seemed to bleed on the woods silhouetted at the far side of the green.

A fine drizzle started. The committee finished their task and quickly dispersed. Ella pressed back against the wall of the pub and quickly stowed her camera in its waterproof bag, stuffing the petals down the front of her blouse. Then she called out to the last of the retreating women, 'Susan!' and dashed over the road.

Susan zipped her track-suit top right up to the collar and hurried back across the road.

'What's the matter?' She stopped dead as soon as she reached the green. 'Oh, it's you!'

Ella crouched low to the ground in front of the dressing, pulled her blouse up out of her skirt at the front and shook her breasts. Silvery leaves and petals fluttered to the ground like confetti. Susan watched as though transfixed. It was quite dark now, a single street light fifty yards away barely penetrating the curtain of drizzle across the open green. But Ella could tell that for the first time Susan was really looking at her.

'Don't worry. I won't bite.'

'No, I suppose not,' Susan said, with a giggle covering a tone of voice which almost said she wished Ella would.

'Do you want to help?'

Ella had called out to Susan on impulse. A prank like this was more exciting if there was a witness. She never imagined she'd make her an accomplice. But Susan eagerly bent down and picked up a handful of the silver petals.

'I'm going to add a mermaid,' Ella said.

Susan giggled again, like a cheeky schoolgirl.

Something is happening here, Ella thought. She smiled to herself as she cleared a space by the river on the picture and blocked out the shape of her mermaid with her fingernail.

'I'll do the bottom half,' Susan volunteered. 'That's easy.'

They worked alongside each other but Ella couldn't concentrate. She kept glancing sideways. Susan's face glistened in the wet, only inches away. Droplets of water gathered on the end of her angelic nose, backlit against the distant streetlight, and either dropped unnoticed, or were shaken sideways with a laugh. Occasionally her tongue shot out and teased the drop into her mouth, as if she was thirsty.

This was a new Susan. Her every movement breathed desire.

'I can't get the breasts right,' she muttered.

'You need a model to work from,' Susan said. She stepped back half a pace and her eyes came up to fix on Ella's in a deep, compelling gaze. Slowly she unzipped her top and took it off; pulled her T-shirt up over her head and tossed it to the ground beside her; unhooked her bra and cast it away. Then she broke the chill, lustful stare and leaned back, her neck exposed in a long convex arch, her small high breasts stretched and staring at the sky. She shook her hair and came back to the vertical smiling. Now her creamy white chest was glistening with the fine warm rain, with larger droplets forming on the ends of the brown nipples. Ella reached forward with one hand to touch them lightly, to release the rain, and she lingered there with the gentlest of caresses.

'They are exquisite,' she said.

Susan's lips parted and moved silently. She was going to

say something about being too small, or too unknowing, Ella guessed. She sensed a slight tremor of pent-up desire not yet clear of its former wrapping in layers of shyness and fear of the forbidden. She responded by meeting the quivering, uncertain lips with the rich assurance of her own.

The soft thin lips did not withdraw from Ella. They became still. But they did not move to meet her. So Ella pressed against them gingerly, and at the same time probed with the moist tip of her tongue. She ran it around the line of her own lips, and then made contact with Susan's. At the same time she brought her chest up against the naked breasts and let them touch. She could feel the other heart pounding in its pearly ribcage.

Then she slid her tongue forward into the other mouth. It opened like a magic door, as sweet with gifts as Aladdin's cave, and Ella's tongue swept on its sensual search until it met and rejoiced with Susan's. The girl kissed her back with a freshness and vigour which made Ella gasp and grip her body tighter. The passion of their sudden meeting took both by surprise. Susan started to fall backwards. Ella put a hand behind her and leaned over to pull her forwards, but she was too late. Susan fell, with Ella on top of her.

For a moment they lay there on the wet grass in each others' arms, kissing deeply. Ella rolled on to her back, pulling Susan on top of her. The scent of the drenched earth was divine, and as she lunged into Susan's mouth she reached round to grab her bottom and press it down against her. The jeans were sodden and Susan struggled away and stood up, pulling the material away from the cleft to which it was stuck.

'Ugh!' she said. 'I'm caked with mud.'

Ella wanted to pull her back down and cake her breasts as well, to roll naked with her in the patch without grass where the cricket crease had been. She started to unbutton her own sopping blouse and her breasts burst out, engorged and erect with arousal. They seemed enormous to Susan, flooding her again with a sense of her own girlishness, for all their similarity of age.

'Oh dear,' she said shamefaced. 'Oh dear!'

Ella put a hand up to Susan's crotch and could feel the pressure of the pee coming out. She was like a little nervous, excited kitten.

Ella rose to her feet, reading correctly the girl's doubts and daring. 'Don't worry,' she said, taking her hand in a matronly way. 'Your whole body is an invitation to sex. I'll show you how.'

The headlights of a solitary car swept over the far end of the green as it turned on to the road beside them.

'Quick!' Ella said, pulling Susan by the hand and running away from the village into the pitch blackness at the centre of the green. The car sped on its route and the sound of its engine faded from hearing, leaving them only with the racing of their two hearts. Susan collapsed on to the grass, panting. The rain had stopped and the wet ground seemed to steam as the heat of the previous day lapped up the liquid refreshment of the night.

Ella crouched at Susan's feet and pulled off her pixie boots. She rolled the thin cotton socks down over her ankles, tugged them off by the toes, and stuffed them into the boots. Then she loosened her belt and unfastened the waist button. She knelt at the girl's side and pushed one hand down the front of her jeans into the panties she felt there, to nestle in the small patch of dank hair. At the same time she lowered her mouth on to the nearest nipple and kissed it.

As the breasts rose up to meet her, Ella ran her tongue in circles round the nipple and then flicked it from side to side. She sucked hard, then very gently caught it between her teeth and pretended to bite it. Susan began to whimper with a passion and Ella responded by sucking hard, taking almost all of the tit in her mouth. She held it up from the chest with her spare hand and sucked deeply and rhythmically, as though she were milking her.

Susan began to gasp with tormented pleasure as Ella abandoned the first breast and leaned over to minister to the second. Susan thrust her chest up to meet the mouth, at the same time raising her hips against the hand in her crotch.

'Easy, easy,' Ella said soothingly. 'Take your time . . .'

'But I want it! I want it!'

'And you shall have it, sweetheart . . .'

Ella took a firm hold of the jeans at the waist and tugged them forcibly over hips and abdomen, crotch, thighs, knees, calves . . . and off her lovely little feet. One naked thigh half crossed the other in a spontaneous gesture of modesty. Ella could just see the tiny triangle of black hair. She paused to slide out of her own skirt and Susan rolled over and over in the rough wet grass, as if to get away from her.

Then Ella pounced. She grabbed hold of the two legs, drenched again now as if with dew, and held them stationary. She wrenched the thighs apart, kneeling between them, went down on the cunt, and thrust her tongue straight up inside it.

Then she came out, as she recalled the fantasy she had shared with Susan.

The girl gave a little cry of surprise, more at the coming out than the going in, Ella thought. She briefly kissed the hidden button at the top of the vaginal opening and began to mimic the art teacher's genital massage. In the dark it was all by feel, and she condensed the strokes. She took a tiny clump of pubic hair in her teeth, stretched it out, tugged, and let go. Then another clump. At the same time her index finger traced the line of the outer labia. She could feel them engorge with the stimulation. Then round the inner lips. They swelled too, and separated. She dipped inside with her finger to feel the juiciness. And with her finger now lubricated she swept around the hood of the clitoris, gradually pushing it back until the very bud of her rose was exposed, thrusting and tight and indescribably intent.

Susan groaned desperately.

Ella let go of the hair and slid her tongue down to the clitoris, licking it from side to side as it grew tighter, harder, greedier. She swung one of her own legs over one of Susan's, sliding her own cunt up and down the arch of the tiny foot as she licked at Susan's cunt. She fell into a rhythm: a deep thrust into the vagina then up to swirl around the clitoris, then deep inside again, as her own cunt rubbed up against the ankle then slipped down to the toes.

Susan's hips began to move up and down, locked in the same rhythm. The knee which was pressed against Ella's abdomen rose and fell. The foot which was unknowingly fucking Ella's clitoris arched, pressed, and slid away incessantly.

'Oh! . . . I can't stop . . . I can't stop it . . .'

'Ride it! Ride it!' Ella whispered firmly. And as Susan's hips forced her cunt even harder against Ella's tongue, the experienced woman moved her hands under the firm little bottom, grabbed its cheeks, squeezed them, rolled them, forced them apart . . . pushing ever upwards as her tongue forced down.

'It's coming . . .'

Ella placed one finger against the tiny rose hole of Susan's bottom and pressed the very tip of it inside. She felt the muscle grip her for dear life. Then she pursed her lips around the clitoris and sucked strongly as her tongue kept on stroking it from side to side. Two fingers of her other hand plunged into the vagina.

'Oh! Oh! Oh!'

The crotch jerked a foot higher off the ground then wrenched to one side. It shuddered quickly and twisted back. Three or four times it writhed from side to side, pinioned by fingers in both holes and a mouth at the pinnacle.

As the panicky noise subsided into controlled gentle groans, Ella gradually let the centre of the body lower itself to the ground. Barely touching, she stroked the outer thighs. She planted soft kisses randomly in soft places. Every now and then Susan would kick out with an electric spasm, or shake her arms involuntarily and gasp with relief. And her bosom heaved.

Ella was patient, loving.

At last Susan stirred herself back into consciousness.

'What about you?' she said with gratitude but also some effort.

'You could simply do for me whatever felt good to you,' Ella answered, wanting to empower the girl. 'But your lovely little body has given me so much pleasure already, I can come very quickly without you instigating anything. Just lie back and let me ravish myself on you.'

She knelt up, lifted Susan's foot by the heel and pressed the ball of it against her vulva. Susan wriggled her toes obligingly as Ella rubbed herself against them. Then Ella moved up, straddling Susan's middle, mingling thatch with thatch and swaddling Susan's tender clitoris in her own lower lips. Susan flinched at first and Ella drowned the rawness of the contact by opening her labia with her fingers and rubbing her own lubricating juices over both of their cunts. Then up again, creeping forward with a knee on each side until she could bring her cunt down on each pert breast. She fucked them both in turn. Then on again. She heard Susan inhale deeply with joyful surprise at the scent of her as at last she straddled her face.

'Your tongue,' Ella whispered, asking.

She felt it enter her, small and tentative. She dropped down on it and fucked. It grew bolder and longer as it searched inside her. Ella leaned forward and rubbed her clitoris against Susan's nose. She was going to blow in seconds.

But there was another surprise for her. Susan reached up and swiftly fondled her breasts. Her hands moved quickly down Ella's waist, perhaps sensing the galloping speed of events. They swept round to Ella's bottom, grabbed the cheeks, and sank their nails into the flesh as Ella spent her force. She had to lift herself, or she would have smothered the girl in the enthusiasm of her orgasm. But in doing so she felt a magnificent communion with the greater world, the grass, the wetness, the village, the night . . .

Soon they would get cold and have to move, Ella knew. But there was time first to marvel at the experience. There was the fantasy, just as there had been with the cricket. There was frustration at the sexual apathy. And then, in both instances, there was the village green, where her frustration exploded in the most incredible, urgent, uninhibited sex. What on earth was going on?

4

ON THE BEATEN PATH

'What the hell is going on?'

The man kept the radiophone to his ear as he listened to the reply, but switched his attention to a can of Coors beer in his other hand. He was wearing a business suit and a weather-stained ten-gallon hat complete with a sash made of Indian beads and two eagle feathers.

'What the hell d'you mean, you don't goddamned know? I bought you a castle, didn't I? Why the screamin' mercies d'you think I set you up in the goddamned castle?'

He flicked a switch on his armrest and the heavily tinted rear window of his customised Cadillac Eldorado slid down smoothly. He spat vigorously into Park Lane.

'Close the window,' he told the chauffeur in front of him. 'Then take me to Pod Whatsit.'

He leaned back and finished the beer. He gave the empty can to the personal assistant beside him, and then put his hand on her knee and stroked her thigh as he continued his telephone conversation.

'Ah've got clients begging to throw billions of bucks at the biggest breakthrough in communications this century, all riding on this here Pod prototype. And I'm damned sure I'm not gonna let it all slip away because of some damned fool game of cricket . . .'

He pushed his PA's mock-Indian miniskirt up to her crotch and rubbed his hand against the triangle of jet-black hair which fluffed out her silk panties.

'I know they weren't playing goddamned cricket last night! So find out what the hell they *were* playing . . . And *who* was playing . . . And how they managed to lose us so much goddamned energy for the second goddamned time!'

The PA took the phone from him and spread her legs apart. But he suddenly changed his mind and withdrew his hand.

'Business first,' he said gruffly. 'How long till we reach this Pod place?'

'About two hours.' She crossed her legs demurely and pulled her skirt back down to cover her crotch.

'Let's see the TV, honey.'

She leaned forward and unzipped the back of the passenger seat, revealing a twenty-four-inch screen supported by state of the art technology. She passed him another can of Coors.

'And get out the controls . . .'

She handed over the machine's remote control and then unzipped his fly and reached in. She manoeuvred his large but flaccid penis out of his underpants and trousers then retreated to her side of the seat and took out a notepad and pencil.

He switched channels frantically. He took a big swig of beer, then more channels. He flashed through half a dozen European languages, becoming more and more agitated. At last he hit an advert, and stopped.

Women in fishnet stockings and high heels were draping themselves over a new model car. They did nothing for him. Neither did the woman with the gorgeous ass and a new brand of shampoo. He pushed back his cowboy hat and frowned.

Then the camera panned a supermarket shelf and the voice-over described the virtues of a certain brand of canned tomatoes. His penis lurched. It stiffened, and he smiled. It stood out half, two-thirds, three-quarters of a foot or more from his business suit and he couldn't keep his hand off it. He started rubbing himself, sliding the outer skin up and down.

Then a programme started.

'Damned fine commercial,' he said with a huge grin. 'Give it eighty-five.'

His secretary made a note of the time and channel, and the mark out of a hundred which her boss had awarded the advert.

He ran through the channels again until he found more commercials. A new formula floor polish . . . his cock pulsed to life again, the foreskin stretched as tight as a drumskin.

'Eighty-seven.'

The secretary jotted it down.

A building society advertised their services with an aerial shot of a big city and blood throbbed along the rugged vein running the length of his shaft. He stroked it up and down and grunted with pleasure.

'Ninety-one.'

He wanked his way right up the M1 and across the M6 and on to the A-road and down the B-road towards his destination, dipping into satellite TV channels right across Europe looking for the ads that gave him a charge, and grading them out of a hundred. He was tireless and happy.

'It's money in the bank,' he kept saying between surges of gluttonous wanking. 'Money in the bank.'

Then came one for a breakfast cereal. He couldn't have said what it was about the product or the sales pitch – not the shape of the packet, or the colour of the table it sat on, and certainly not the close-up of the hand which grasped the packet and tipped it into the bowl – but something here grabbed him totally and irresistibly. He was almost delirious with greed and pleasure.

'Money in the bank,' he drooled.

His secretary leaned over with a napkin and wiped a tiny dribble of saliva from the corner of his mouth.

'Goddammit, it's too much!' he cursed. His hand moved faster and faster up and down, finally out of his control. 'I'll get my suit wet!'

The car swung off the road suddenly, passing through a gate in a high brick wall.

The secretary pushed her boss's hand from his cock and replaced it with her own. Then she leaned over and took the glans efficiently and entirely into her mouth.

The chauffeur wound down his window and paused at the lodge gate.

'Mr Carnel,' he announced.

A uniformed security guard peered through the tinted rear window and then waved the car on.

The secretary sucked hard and the boss pumped his sperm into her mouth.

Gravel crunched under the wheels as the car sped up the driveway of Pod Manor.

She kept sucking and pumping his shaft with her hand until she had extracted and swallowed the very last drops of sperm. While it was still erect she licked carefully round the tip with her tongue and dried it with her lips. Then as it crumpled she stuffed it back into the trousers, tucked it inside the underpants, fastened the zip and smoothed the clean dry fabric with her hand.

'Ninety-nine!' said Blas Carnel with smug satisfaction as the cereal ad finished and the car came to a halt. 'And ninety-nine for you too, my little chickadee.' He patronised the girl's thigh with a hearty slap. Then he hauled his two hundred and fifty pounds out of the car, straightened his enormous hat, and strode into the house to take emergency control of field operations.

'What the dickens is going on?' Ella demanded.

'You're picking up some good English idioms, for one thing,' Goode said.

'Yesterday you wouldn't so much as put your head inside and now you're throwing pebbles on my bedroom window and banging the door down.'

'Hurry up. Put these on.' He tossed a pair of thick woollen socks over the threshold and plonked a pair of hiking boots on the back step. 'You must have had a late night.'

'I was paying tribute to the water gods,' Ella answered.

'Well it's the land gods today, and then they both come together with hymns on the green.'

Ella stretched Goode's thick-knit stockings into shape as though she were breaking open a new packet of nylons. Then she cramped each one up in turn, with her thumbs inside, set her foot on the edge of a chair, and drew it evocatively around her toes. She slowly unfurled it, smoothing the fabric up her calf to the knee.

'I love cross-dressing,' she said seductively.

'*I'm* going after a pair of lesser whitethroats in a dry beechwood,' he answered plainly. 'But you're beating the bounds, and the route gets tough and boggy.'

'And you didn't want me to spoil my incredibly sexy Roman sandals.' Ella enjoyed her unrequited flirtation with the gentleman bird spotter. 'I expect I'll come back all hot and sweaty, with steam billowing up out of the lace holes.'

On the way to the starting point at the far side of the village Goode quickly filled her in.

'In the days of Richard de Pode there were no walls or fences. And no maps. So once a year the villagers walked round the fields and commons in the company of the chief bailiff, who patched up any quarrels about the land which may have cropped up since the last walk.'

'And beat the bounders?' Ella asked.

'No, beat the impressionable youngsters. They were knocked against boundary stones, thrown into ponds and streams and pushed into ditches, brambles and nettles wherever they crossed the line. The idea was to make such an impression on them that for the rest of their lives they would know exactly where the boundary lay.'

Ella's feet might be well protected, but the rest of her body sported only a thin cotton T-shirt and hot pants.

'Do I count as an elder or a youngster?' she asked dubiously.

'Nowadays the kids carry fresh cut willow wands, or garden canes if they're lazy, and beat the boundary stones instead.'

'Progress,' Ella said, still with a sense of doubt.

They had missed the start, but Goode knew a short cut and drew a map to show Ella how she could head them off. If she lost her way she could simply follow her ears, because the beaters were making an unearthly racket with drums, kazoos and whistles as they proceeded.

'The vicar goes round with them to ask God's blessing on the crops,' Goode explained. 'But the pagan way was to make a din to show the nasties you mean business.'

And as usual, the pagan way is more fun, Ella thought. She loved how the pagan cohabited in these village customs, stripped of menace but still rich with a sense of earthiness and crudity.

As she hurried down the farmtrack towards the drumming noise, for instance, Ella could not help but picture a culminating concert of awesome percussion on the village green, with herself as guest conductor. The orchestra would be paired at each music stand and as she raised her baton to bring them in together, one from each pair would stand, drop his trousers or raise her skirt and lay across the lap of the other. Ah, what thrilling rhythms! What inspiration from the rostrum! Her artistry would know no bounds!

In the distance Ella heard a commanding voice shout, 'Whack it, gang! Whack it!' And she came quickly to her senses. If her current fantasy was going to become reality the moment they reached the green, she had better make sure it was something she could keep manageable. She felt she owed it to the neighbours.

So she hurried on, hoping soon to latch her thoughts on to one particular person. Susan perhaps. Or the vicar . . .

But when she caught up, all the familiar frustrations returned. Nobody seemed the slightest bit interested in her, no matter how much she flirted or flaunted her body. The beating of the boundary stones was a pathetic pantomime devoid of any real passion. Even the din was a soulless one. It gave her a headache.

Susan wasn't there. Ella thought she recognised some of her admirers from the cricket team but any ardour they may have felt belonged to another time and place. Then she spotted the scorer, the gawky adolescent who had already spurned her in the upstairs room of the teahouse. He would be the target for her fantasy, she decided. She would wreak her vengeance. She would teach him a lesson he would never forget until the day he died. She would show him where some other boundaries lay, some other boundaries at the frontiers of his experience.

Ella smiled for the first time since joining the gang. When they stopped for one of their dirgelike songs she picked a small wild rose from the hedgerow, set it in her hair, and took a few pictures of herself with the Minolta on time-delay, lodged in a thicket.

First I'll need to know where he's coming from, she told herself as she fell into single file behind him to cross a field of ripe corn. I'll strip him naked. And after I've scrutinised his working parts I'll survey the boundaries of his experience. I'll beat it out of him if necessary. Then I'll know what to build on.

They passed through a muddy farmyard.

He'll need to learn some chivalry, for one thing. I shall be Queen and he shall be my Walter Raleigh. And if he has no velvet cloak to throw over the mud so I do not get my boots dirty, then he shall use his own naked body!

Where the farm track joined the lane there was a cattle grid. People clustered round one of the gateposts and again a man called out 'Whack it, gang! Whack it!'

Ella reached for the gawky youth's stick.

'Can I have a go?' She wanted to show this feeble lot what a real whack was like.

But he pulled his five-foot length of willow away from her.

'No. It's mine! You should have brought your own.'

Ella walked over the cattle grid slowly and deliberately, stepping on every bar. She imagined it as a rack. 'People like you should be stretched out and exposed,' she muttered under her breath. 'Until they've agreed to let a little sunshine in.'

The route passed along the edge of a copse and Ella pushed her way through a gap in the hedge to pull off a long shoot from a willow stool. She scratched herself down one leg and notched up another grudge against her selfish young man. She caught up with him and tugged at his sleeve.

'Will you lend me your pocket knife?'

He looked disparagingly at her tatty stick and then reluctantly dug into his pocket and handed her a penknife.

'Give it back as soon as you've finished,' he said.

She kept up with him as she worked on the stick. She cut it down to about three feet, which was half the size of the others. She trimmed off the side branches, which left tiny knots along its length. And she pared off the bark, leaving the stick moist and shiny. It was a good half-inch thick at one end but tapered away at the other. It was pliant when she pressed it against the palm of her hand; it cut through the air like a whip when she swished it.

By the time she had prepared the switch to her satisfaction, the gang had gathered round a milestone. It lay close beneath a hawthorn hedge, and they had to bunch together closely to reach it. Ella stuck close by her man but held her stick behind her back.

'Aren't you going to use it then?' he asked.

She leaned forward with the others and whispered in his ear: 'I'm keeping it for your little stone bum.'

He made no immediate sign that he had heard. But as the walk resumed he niftily manoeuvred himself away from her. If she held herself back a little from the crowd, he would soon be at the front. If she caught up and went into the lead, he would drop back. And he made sure she never caught his eye.

Ella was beginning to enjoy herself. She lingered lovingly over a patch of honeysuckle in the hedgerow. When the gang stopped to perform, she picked dandelion clocks and blew the seed to all points of the compass. When they made their pagan din she slapped her switch down against the side of her hiking boot.

And at last they came back to the village. A crowd gathered round the well-dressing, which had aged beautifully over the last few days. The colours had faded. Some wilted blooms, like creases round the eyes, gave it the stature of experience. And the clay had dried and cracked with the majesty of an old master.

Ella avoided the green, watching the final ceremony from the sexual safety of the road in front of the pub. When it was over and people dispersed to their homes, she crossed the road and strolled smartly past her target bounder.

'Don't you want your penknife back?' she asked.

'Hey!' he shouted, rifling through his trousers pockets as he remembered. 'Yeah!'

But she didn't stop.

'Wait! 'Course I want it back.'

He ran to catch up. She turned to face him just as he came level with her.

'You'll have to be more polite than that!'

She waited long enough to note his confusion and then continued walking away from him at a slower pace. He followed her further on to the green.

'Yes,' he said, uncomfortably. 'Yes, of course. Please . . .'

'Please what?'

'Please, my penknife.'

She stopped again and gave him a long seductive smile with a suggestion of condescension turning gradually to reproach. He turned bright red and hung his head.

'Please, miss.'

'That's better.' A look of triumph spread across her face as she realised that the magic was at work. The space between them was supercharged with sexual force. She could sense his sleepy, gawkish penis awakening, like an animal of unknown strength and habit surfacing after a long hibernation in a strange lair.

'But I would like to find somewhere a little more private to repay you properly.'

'You would?' he gulped.

Her encouraging smile changed quickly to a disapproving frown.

'I mean,' he stuttered. 'I mean, you would, miss? I mean, please . . . I mean, thank you, miss.'

She dangled the little penknife in front of him, drawing him towards the woods at the far side.

'For the loan of the knife,' she said, her smile returning. Then with the subtlest hint of a curl at the corner of her full-blooded upper lip she added: 'And for all your selfish slights and rudeness.'

He hung his head again, thrilled at the prospect of any reward from this female goddess, any reward at all, but at the same time terrified of causing more offence.

'Yes, miss,' he muttered.

'Yes, Miss Deedes,' she said.

'Yes, Miss Deedes.'

Ella scanned the wood ahead. She was wary of leaving the green, not knowing if the magic of her fantasy world would still keep him in her sexual power. There were only a few people left round the well-dressing and they showed no sign of straying from the roadside. But it was broad daylight, and she wanted absolute control.

'There's a dip over there, where we drained the pond, Miss Deedes.' Her charge pointed to the far corner where green, wood, and corn field met. But she did not look.

'Your advice was not sought,' she snapped.

'Sorry, Miss Deedes.'

'Yes, so am I. Very sorry indeed. It means you have no idea where your boundaries lie. You must not talk unless you are invited. I shall have to teach you in such a way that you never forget . . .'

She decided to probe her power further.

'. . . With my cane!'

She marched away in the direction he had pointed and held her breath until she was certain he was following. Then without turning round she commanded him: 'You will walk three paces behind me. With your eyes on my feet.' And she knew beyond doubt that he was obeying her.

The dip was roughly circular, about forty feet in diameter and with steep sides falling to a depth of almost five feet. It was perfectly dry and they were entirely hidden from the village.

'Do you still want your reward?' she asked.

'Yes, please, Miss Deedes,' he answered sheepishly.

'Then you must learn your lesson first. You must touch your toes so I can make a lasting impression on you!'

He bent down and his trousers stretched tight over his bottom revealing the shape of his cheeks with his balls nicely framed between them. Ella traced the outline gently with her hand, marvelling as she never tired of doing at the varied splendour of Eros. This was a game for the outskirts of the village and the edge of the pagan. But they would play in the open air and under the broad sun! She would enjoy her playful revenge and she would take her pleasure as the mood took her. But she knew from the eagerness of his tight little bottom and bulging balls that she would be giving pleasure too. She would stretch the boundaries of his selfish, narrow world with a new definition of give and take!

'What do the beaters say at the boundary?' she asked him.

' "Whack it!" Miss Deedes. "Whack it!" '

Ella swished her cane down across his cheeks. She reached her left hand underneath his belly to feel his cock. It was as stiff as a poker.

She let go of it.

'Whack it, miss. Whack it!' he begged.

'That obviously won't make a lasting impression,' she said. 'Take off your trousers.'

In her adopted role of strict mistress she found his gratification too obvious and immediate for her liking, and his reflex erection tactless. He stepped out of his trousers gleefully and she ordered him again to look only at her feet.

He was wearing Y-fronts.

'Off with the shirt!'

He kept his eyes on the ground. Did he know, she wondered, that the tip of his cock was sticking out of the waistband of his underpants? It was a long thin one. Wiry and energetic, she hoped.

'Bend over again!'

Now he must know. The tip of his cock was pressing against his abdomen, jabbing his belly-button. The thin white cotton of his Y-fronts stretched across the slit between his cheeks like an artist's virgin canvas awaiting the master's designs.

Ella pressed her left hand against the fabric stretched over the ramrod between his legs and brought her right hand down sharply against his cheeks. She felt his cock lurch forward against the one hand as the other came down harder and harder. Six vigorous spanks. Then she ordered him out of the rest of his clothes.

He kept his eyes on her feet as he stripped. Then he stood two paces in front of her, his head bent but his cock so vertical in its uncontrollable reaction to his predicament that it stood flush with the tight, downy skin of his abdomen.

Ella rocked forward and back slightly in her boots.

'You may kiss them,' she said.

Without hesitation he went down on his knees before her

and touched his lips adoringly to the toes of her boots, each in turn. He kissed his way up her laces. He lingered worshipfully at the small piece of soft leather which protruded above the tie and nestled against the front of her strong ankle, so that it became a French kiss between the tip of the boot's tongue and his own.

'And where has this heathen passion come from?' Ella asked.

'I don't know what you mean, miss.'

Ella raised one foot and placed it on his shoulder, the thick sole of the hiking boot pressing into his naked flesh. She pushed him over and pinned him to the ground on his back with her foot on his bare chest. No hair there yet, she observed. Cock as stiff as ever.

'Who's your girlfriend?' she asked.

'I haven't got one, Miss Deedes.'

She leaned forward, putting more weight on his chest and snarled at him: 'Don't lie to me, footman!'

'Honestly, Miss Deedes!' He squirmed uncomfortably. 'It's the truth!'

With the end of her cane, Ella tapped reprovingly along each of his thighs. 'Boyfriends?'

He shook his head.

She slid the tip of her cane between his penis and abdomen and pried the stiff rod out. 'You play with yourself?'

'No,'

She let go of it with her cane and it sprang back, slapping hard against his belly.

'I mean with this.' She poked his cock to the side and again it sprang back. This time she caught a faint scent of it. 'What do you call it?' she asked.

He hesitated and she struck his upper thigh harder with the cane.

'My dick,' he said hurriedly.

'Good,' Ella said. 'I like your dick. You dick is asking to be played with. Turn over.' She pushed him with her foot. 'On your hands and knees!'

She reached under his belly, grabbed his dick in her left hand and squeezed it. It was undaunted, its vigour unquenchable. She slowly slid her hand up and down its length.

'Your dick likes being played with very much,' she said. Then she brought the cane down with all her strength across both his cheeks, leaving an angry red stripe across his flesh. He squealed and flinched away from her, but she had him by the dick in her other hand. She held him tight, and then went on stroking.

'So why don't you play with him?'

'I used to, Miss Deedes.'

She caned him again, making a red cross on his bottom.

'Why didn't you let me play with him when I wanted to?'

'I am doing now, Miss Deedes,' he whimpered pathetically. 'I want you to now!'

It was true enough, and Ella thought it time to loosen up on the rules. But she was enjoying the role-play too much to abandon it completely.

'Up you get,' she said. 'But before our final ceremony, we have a few obstacles to manoeuvre.' She reached for her camera and then sat with her legs bent at the knees and ordered him: 'Through the gap in the hedge!'

He went down on his belly and wriggled his way through, his cock brushing the ground and his bottom collecting a couple of playful smacks as he did so.

Ella stood with one foot almost horizontal against the bank and ordered him 'over the stile'. As soon as he had one leg over she carefully raised her knee, pressing it gently upwards into his bottom and making him stretch up high on his toes, his dick ever at attention.

She playfully moulded her body into a semblance of different land forms and barriers and ordered him over, under, round or through them as she shot off a roll of film. She feasted on the spectacle of his naked body with its cane-kissed bottom and its ever-stiff cock in bizarre positions. She prodded, poked and penetrated as the mood took her. The slightest hesitation on his part and he was accused of disobedience. He admitted his guilt. He pleaded for punishment.

The distinct angry lines of the cane across his bottom

became a generalised red glow. And the hotter she made him, the hotter she became herself. She pinned him to the earth suddenly, with a foot on his chest.

'Time to pay homage at the well,' she said.

She stood above him, one foot on each side of his cock, and he instinctively stretched himself out, feet together and hands way above his head as though on a rack. Ella was still wearing her T-shirt and hot pants, and Goode's hiking boots and thick stockings. She took the penknife from her pocket, opened the blade, and carefully unpicked a length of the seam of her pants. She made a slit just big enough for his cock, opposite the opening of her cunt. She wore no knickers underneath.

She smiled at her young footman, who was still straining to keep his eyes on her boots.

'I've seen enough of your spotty face,' she laughed as she tossed the penknife aside and turned to face his feet. She knelt above his tireless organ, one knee on either side of his thighs. She held the slit in her pants open with one hand and took hold of his dick with the other. She lowered her crotch further and guided the tip of his dick through the fabric, between her labia and into her vagina. She rocked up and down a little, to lubricate his rod with her juices, making sure he didn't slip out. Then she sank right down on top of him, gripped his naked flanks with her booted ankles as if she were on a horse, and began riding him in earnest.

But long before she had reached a gallop, before she had even broken into a trot, with its lovely rhythm of rise and fall, she felt the dick inside her surge and leap. The base pressed hard against her pelvic bone while the tip of it, deep inside her, bobbed and shook like a stallion with its head in halter for the first time. She could feel the hot sperm squirting out of him and it brought her on rapidly, despite her fury at his presumption.

She gripped his dick tightly with her pelvic muscles, determined to keep it big inside her. In one fast movement she lay down flat on top of him, head to toe, forcing the cock which was trapped inside her down at an unnatural angle. He grunted with shock, surprise, pleasure; she didn't stop to analyse as she rolled over sideways and pulled him up on top of her.

'Don't you dare move!'

'I won't, Miss Deedes.' He was like a puppy told off for something he didn't understand. He kissed the tongues of her boots again, desperate to make amends and knowing only how to repeat what had gone before.

His dick was still stiff inside her. Young and wily, she told herself reassuringly. But she wasn't taking any chances. He was on top of her now, head to toe, making love to her boots with his face. And his athletic cock was bent back at an unnatural angle, lodged up her cunt. So far so good. But if he lifted himself he might come out and not fit back in. And she couldn't get enough motion from underneath.

She pushed his legs apart by thirty degrees, one each side of her, and looked down at their point of union for inspiration. There was his rosy red bum framing his two big balls. They were squashed against her thatch of curly pubic hair, obliterating any further view of operations. She stroked the thin, downy hair which half enveloped them, and followed the line of fluff up the crack of his bottom.

'We're a bit off the beaten path, my hasty but valiant footman.'

'Yes ma'am.'

'But rescue is at hand.' She brought the flat of her right hand down on the tender flesh of his right cheek in a resounding slap and felt his dick lurch deeper inside her. There was just enough movement against her clitoris. She brought her left palm down on the other side of his bottom and his organ lurched again. A little dart of keen sensation flew from hand to bum to cock and ricocheted around her genitals before breaking itself on her clitoris. Her hand came down again and again. The darts came in a shower. He was slobbering over her feet. And then he tried to push up against her hand. She smacked him down harder. But back he came, begging for it. He was fucking her again, she realised. He begged her to keep going, to keep whacking his bottom. She was keeping him inside. She was firing the darts, but she was starting to shoot wild. She rained down blow after blow. But she lost her aim. She slapped his thighs. She caught the underhang of his bottom with her nails. She scratched his flesh. She poked and jabbed. Then she saw his balls tighten and sensed them fire . . . she grabbed on to his bum and went with it, squeezed him and shuddered, shuddered, shuddered as he shot his sperm into her for the second time.

The lad seemed to be in a sort of stupor for a while. Ella rounded up his clothes and helped to dress him. She put his pocket knife into his fist and curled his fingers round it. He grinned at her like a Cheshire cat.

'You said you *used* to play with your dick,' Ella said. 'Why did you stop?'

'I don't know,' he answered, still smiling gormlessly. 'I just sort of went off it. I started feeling too drained. It was a long time ago.' And then, as if the timing of it had just occurred to him he added: 'When I was working on the green.'

Ella perked up her ears.

'What work on the green?'

'Draining it.'

'You mean the pond . . . where are we now?'

'Yes. Only it was a big job. We had to go right round the edge of the green. It took months. Good money though.'

Draining the green and 'feeling sort of drained'. It was too powerful a parallel for there to be no connection! Ella was thrilled with him.

'What do you mean, you went right round the edge?' she jabbered excitedly. 'What were you doing?'

He looked sheepishly at her feet again, but his grin was irrepressible. 'I made the tea.'

Ella smiled back, signalling that the interrogation was over. Just one more question.

'Who was your boss?'

'Some Yank.'

5

LE DÉJEUNER SUR L'HERBE

'He wore a big cowboy hat, indoors and out, as though he was in films.' That was all the barmaid would tell her.

Ella quizzed everyone at the King's Arms.

'He acted as though he owned everybody.'

'A big, stocky man. In a huge hat. You could tell he was stinking rich.'

'He swore like a trooper.'

'A fat blasphemer.'

'A cowboy.'

Not an easy man to miss in Pod Parva, she thought. But he had come to the village only a few times. And no one could put a face to his minions. But some of them still lived at Pod Manor, they thought, and ran their business out of a place in Pod Magna.

Ella popped home to change clothes. She considered her black velvet miniskirt, dark seamed nylons and high heels, construction workers being construction workers the world over. But the Pods being the Pods, and herself being in need of a ride, she switched to a sundress in soft yellow with a laced V-back and full-circle skirt. She slipped back into her white leather sandals with relief and criss-crossed the decorative thongs up the calves of her legs. She took a wicker shopping basket with her to complete the wholesome effect, and hurried out to find someone to drive her. She hailed a passing plumber's van in much the same way that she would have hailed a taxi in Manhattan and he took her, en route for his lunch, straight to the Pod Magna premises of SMIPT Incorporated.

The shopfront sported a display of sink and bath taps, and Ella adopted the guise of prospective customer.

'Sorry sweetie. They're not taps, they're faucets,' said the doll behind the counter. She paused over her Indian beadwork embroidery and smiled sympathetically. 'American things. They wouldn't fit your size pipes.'

'My sockets are universal,' Ella answered. 'They can handle any kind of equipment I want to screw on.' She barged through the back door of the shop into a builder's yard. A very sterile builder's yard. There were a couple of excavators and a dumper truck, their paintwork without a scratch. And a lean-to full of large coils of shiny piping. Or *was* it piping? She dashed over to look, ignoring the girl's shouting and cussing behind her. This was solid piping, made up of alternating layers of different materials, like a sort of cylindrical plywood.

The panicky squealing stopped suddenly and Ella hurried back to the shop. The super salesgirl was babbling frantically into the telephone but clamped up the second Ella returned.

'No sis-butt irrigation systems on sale?' Ella asked.

The young woman shook her head, lost.

'Any other drainage company in town where I could enquire?'

'Up the road, first left, second right, two blocks down.'

So Ella left SMIPT Inc in search of Alfred Higgins and Son, stopping at various points on the way to fill her wicker basket with the makings of a first-class picnic.

Son of Higgins, when finally run to earth, was so taken with the impromptu sex show which was Ella Deedes eating a ripe peach, that he gladly told her everything she asked about the draining of the green at Pod Parva. His Dad had been sub-contracted to drain the pond itself because the fatso cowboy obviously didn't know the first thing about it.

'He just liked to sit up in that big yellow machine of his and give orders.'

He watched Ella catch a dribble of juice escaping from the corner of her mouth.

'It probably gave him a hard-on.'

She tracked the juice along her lips with the tip of her tongue and answered: 'Then judging from the amount of piping he's got stockpiled, he must be planning one hell of an orgy.'

Ella was buzzing with excitement, and at times like this it was natural for her to think sex. Sex came to her body as a smile came to her face. It was the fleshy bliss of life and she was too generous a spirit to pinch it back.

But here was her plumber, her lift back to the village.

'*He* can't see beyond sagging ballcocks,' whispered son of Higgins, eager to share a peach or two with Ella in the back of the storeroom.

Nevertheless, thought Ella, the plumber's denim boiler suit was special. She used to have one just like it herself. She had cut out the pockets and worn it without knickers, so she could reach in and play with herself. It was so loose no one could tell. She used to love standing in front of her sour teacher, or a preachy neighbour, with a finger up herself. Or she'd find a big audience, like at a show before the curtain went up or on a crowded station platform, and she'd stand right in front of everyone and frig herself.

She got back into the plumber's van. He hadn't had his lunch yet. So Ella invited him to share her picnic . . . on the village green in Pod Parva. As he considered his answer she craftily reached across the handbrake and slid her hand into the pocket of his dungarees.

In a windowless room at the heart of Pod Manor, Blas Carnel scrutinised a sheaf of computer printout and cussed.

'Goddammit! From three mega-Reichs to absolute goddamned zero in one goddamn morning! What the hell happened out there?'

His personal assistant had switched from her fantasy Cheyenne-squaw outfit to an Annie Oakley equivalent. She was still wearing a leather miniskirt and low-cut top awash with fringes and tassels, but the beadwork had changed to sheriff's stars and the wrinkled buffalo-hide boots to a pair made from stiff leather with sharp toes, three-inch heels and spurs. She took the scarlet kerchief from her neck and mopped her boss's brow.

'Now it's up to five milli-Reichs . . . five measly milli-Reichs! We'll be out of business!'

'Do you want to test it?' the cowgirl asked.

He nodded despairingly and slumped back in his chair, resting his eyes briefly under the brim of an outsize Stetson while she turned on a television set and flipped channels with a remote control. She found some adverts, unzipped his fly and reached in to find his penis. She pulled it out. Lazy, flaccid, unexcited, it still measured six inches long and two inches in diameter. It was a greedy gunslinger of a cock. It lay on his thigh like an unlit cheroot at a poker game.

He flicked the controls and stopped at an advert for cut-price carpets.

'There's something here . . .' he said.

The girl knelt beside him and gently slid the foreskin down, exposing the glans of his penis. She felt a tiny flow of blood into the warm shaft and began masturbating him.

'. . . But not enough to hang a towel on!'

Then the phone rang. It was the shop. A woman from Pod Parva was snooping around.

Carnel's cock lurched and grew.

'It's her!' he said, never one to doubt a hunch that came straight from his cock. 'She's the one that's stealing the sex and costing me money. Follow her!'

He called out a couple of his boys and set them on to the girl with the golden hair in the yellow dress and Roman sandals.

'This is business,' he stressed over the radiophone. 'No pressure, no strong-arm stuff. You just bring her here to me for a little business chat. But make sure she comes.'

Now his excitement was tangible.

'Head, honey. Give me some head!' he told the cowgirl on her knees between his thighs. As she took the thick, stiff cock into her mouth and sucked, he turned his attention back to the phone.

'But whatever you do, don't go out on the green with her. She's dangerous!'

Ella withdrew her hand from the small tight pocket of the

plumber's dungarees. It was full of greasy seals and washers. She wiped herself clean along his inner thigh.

He told her he had his own sandwiches and flask of tea. He always ate in the van, he said, so he could hear the Archers on the radio. And would she keep her hands to herself please because he was driving.

He was a Little Pod man through and through.

Ella turned her thoughts to her monklike minder. She sat back and closed her eyes and pictured a delicious *déjeuner sur l'herbe* with George Goode. She had a cob of rye bread, a piece of Shropshire blue from the centre of the cheese, and a bag of keen French radish; a bottle of Vouvray, *méthode champenoise*; a fresh strawberry tart and a tub of double Devon cream. They would have a brilliant *tête à tête* covering the arts, their personal philosophies and the mating habits of the lesser-spotted birdwatcher and the naturalised rambling rose. Then they would spontaneously move closer and in a moment's silence feel each other's breaths, stretching the silence and then filling it. The bodies quietly touch each other. They can feel the kiss coming. And all the world is strawberry and cream, bubbles, birds and roses, grass and sky . . .

She got out of the plumber's van in front of Goode's cottage and dashed in through the back door without knocking.

Goode was shaving with a cut-throat razor in a tiny mirror over the kitchen sink.

'I'm going up to London,' he explained. 'My lift to the station is coming in ten minutes.'

Ella did a quick calculation. One minute for him to finish shaving. Three minutes to reach the hidden dip on the green and three minutes back. That left three minutes for the sex. She was tempted. She liked the fast ones too. But some trusted inner guide told her that sometimes it was better to take the longer view, and she nobly sacrificed her own immediate pleasure.

'Listen, I've found out what's wrong with the village.'

Goode paused to sharpen his blade on the strop which hung next to the dish towel, and listened.

'The sexual energy of the whole village – men, women,

birds, everyone – is being drained away, I don't know why, by a big American who wears a cowboy hat. The English drained the pond of water, with ordinary pipes, and the Americans drained the rest of the green with special solid plywood-sort-of pipes which takes away everybody's sex drives. I don't know where it goes. It sort of pools somewhere, I guess. I don't know where. But somehow *I* seem to be able to unstop it. And then it floods . . .'

'Have you quite finished?' His voice carried a note of pity which she missed in her excitement.

'No way. Because there's enough of these sex drains stockpiled in a builder's yard in Pod Magna to devastate half the county. And who knows how many good healthy strapping villages have already been drained, dried up, sterilised, castrated . . .'

'You're having problems adapting,' Goode said.

'What about you?' Ella asked. And then she paused and changed track, suddenly suspicious of him. 'Why are you going away? To charge up your own batteries somewhere else?' Her thinking hadn't reached the word conspiracy yet. Was it conceivable that he was involved?

'How do you do it?' she asked. 'Where? How long for?'

'I'm taking a little break. Delivering a few sketches to my agent.' He slapped eau de Cologne on his cheeks and nodded to a leatherbound portfolio beside a bulging holdall on the table.

A car horn sounded in The Row.

Ella decided at once on trust and tactics. 'I'm going to get into Pod Manor somehow or other, to see what's happening here. You are going to be *my* agent in the city. I want to know everything you can find out about SMIPT Inc. Who owns it. Where they're from. What they do.'

The horn beeped insistently.

Goode smiled.

'SMIPT,' he said.

'You'll remember?'

'Yes boss.' He gave her a sweet peck of a kiss on her forehead and fled with his bags.

Ella wandered into the King's Arms with her basket over

her arm and camera round her neck. She recognised the captain of the cricket team, who seemed less of an institution out of his white flannels. He struck her as intelligent, of pleasant humour and extremely handsome. A good substitute for Goode.

'S'cuse me, fella . . .'

It was immediately obvious that Ella appeared to him, too, in a different light. He showed no sign at all of recognising her. She was astonished that he could have blacked out so completely such a recent and uniquely memorable view of her.

'I want to send a picture of myself in England to the folks back home. Would you mind pushing my button?' She handed him her camera as innocently as possible. He took it reluctantly.

'Just outside the pub would be nice, don't you think? In the sunshine . . .'

As she turned to lead him outside, Ella became aware of two thickset young men who had come in behind her. For a moment she regretted her hasty choice. These two could have kept her gainfully occupied all afternoon. But there was something vaguely menacing about them, in a way that came as a shock to her in Pod Parva, and as one of them seemed on the point of offering his services as cameraman she turned back swiftly to her cricketer.

'Maybe we could stand on the edge of the green, with the pub in the background. My folks would just love to see me on a genuine village green.'

The other two pulled back when they heard mention of the green. Ella grabbed her single, grudging assistant by the hand and led him over the road. She showed him how to focus and then posed, instantly imagining herself naked, one hand fondling her breasts and the other her vulva. She was confident of the liberating power of her fantasies once they were on the green, but she wasn't sure that her notion of lunch with Goode would transfer automatically to his substitute.

By the time he had clicked the button her worries were over. She could feel him stripping her through the lens, lingering as he pretended to refocus, and the click came like a jab just where she wanted it.

'Should I take a few more?' he asked eagerly.

'Oh, yes please. But let's walk out a bit further, so we can get those lovely woods in the background.'

He took the picnic basket and offered her his other arm like a gentleman. Ella was positively salivating at the prospect of the feast in front of her.

'This should do,' she said when they had reached the brink of the dip where the pond had been. She moved like a model from one pose to another as she planned the meal ahead and he clicked away.

'Let's show them how suntanned my legs are,' she said, giggling. She ran down to the bottom of the hollow, planted her feet firmly apart and then leaning forward to look down at them she took hold of the fabric of her full-skirted dress a little above the knee and slowly, provocatively lifted it. She hummed seductively as the sandal-ties were revealed at the top of her calves, then her knees, firm and shapely . . . the broadening svelte shafts of her thighs . . . And then at the very point where the converging limbs were about to meet, she stopped and smiled at the camera.

He struggled with the focusing, as if some technical feat of the camera could reveal the thatch of secret hair which nestled behind the hem of her skirt.

He clicked. Then he said hungrily, 'Perhaps your correspondents would like to see how suntanned the backs of your legs are too.'

Ella dropped her skirt, turned around, and this time in absolute silence and even slower, raised her dress from the rear. She could hear his heavy breathing. She stopped when she felt the hem tighten against the underhang of her pantieless bottom. Then she bent down to look back at him upside down with her head between her legs.

'Got to smile at the camera,' she laughed, fully aware that in bending over, the hem of her dress had ridden way above her bottom and that she was giving him a double cheerful peach of a smile. 'And I think you ought to smile back, with the big cheerful joker at the top of *your* legs.'

Ella took firm hold of her ankles and watched through

her legs as the man hurried out of his trousers. His shining jolly cock seemed to guffaw with expectant laughter, jerking from side to side and looming enormous as he came up behind her. It felt burning hot as the tip of it made the first inaccurate contact with the flesh of her bottom. She felt it slide into the cleft between her cheeks. She braced herself, gripping her ankles tightly. Then she felt his hands on her hips, felt the hot rod withdraw. She looked up between her legs and saw the tip of it poised at the entrance to her vagina. It made a few hasty stabs, wide of its target. She felt his hands lift from her, saw one of them grasp the lower end of his shaft, and felt the fingers of the other probing for the entrance to her silken vale. He found it and guided the tip of his cock inside her.

Ella bounced forward and back very slightly to rub her copious juice around the glans of his cock and ease its passage inwards. The hand around it disappeared. He spread his feet apart a little, to bring his genitals down to the same height as hers, and gripped her hips again to steady himself. Then he thrust forward and she watched the thick shaft disappear inside her, until his downy balls kissed her outer lips and she felt his pubic hair scratch against her bottom.

'A picture!' Ella demanded.

'Of the accommodating tourist,' he laughed.

'Of the obliging host!' She tilted forward slightly, withdrawing her lobby from his occupying member until only the head of it was still inside.

'A singular view of the Anglo-American alliance,' he said, as he let go of her waist and fiddled with the camera around his neck.

'The special relationship,' Ella purred as she heard the camera click. But whether it was the sight of his cock poised between her welcoming cheeks with its tip penetrating her vagina, framed in the viewfinder for an audience overseas, or whether it was the irresistible effect of her almost imperceptible tilting forward and back . . . Suddenly he let go of the camera, stammered 'Oh no! Oh no!', and gripped her by her thighs again like a drowning man.

'Enjoy!' Ella told him, thrusting her bum backwards into

his groin until it met his pubes, devouring the whole of his cock. 'Enjoy! Enjoy!'

He thrust his own hips forward against hers, then pumped furiously. But his orgasm had started of its own accord and the come was already well on its way. Within seconds it pooled, sent out its little leaking scout, and then gushed forth like a bursting dam. His pubic bone slammed up against her bottom and stuck there as his penis lurched, stretched, quaked, and propelled its hot elixir hard and fast into the depths of her body.

Ella rhythmically gripped and released his cock with her kegel muscle, draining the sperm from him. Like licking the plate clean, she thought with a smile. Then she slid forward off him, stood up, and dropped her dress neatly back into place.

He looked stunned. A little disappointed perhaps. Even inadequate, she thought.

'Don't worry,' she told him reassuringly. 'You're not supposed to dally over the hors d'oeuvres.' She sat on the grass next to the picnic basket, spread a napkin across her lap and tore off a piece of bread. 'The feast continues.'

He put on his shorts and sat beside her. Ella pulled the hem of her dress up as far as modesty normally allowed, exposing her thighs to the sun. She unfastened the thongs of her sandals and slipped her feet out of them and then popped the cork on the Vouvray.

'No glasses, I'm afraid.' She wiped the neck of the bottle with her napkin and then put it to her lips. With her face lifted to the blue sky, she ran her tongue round the inside of the opening and then pursed her lips precisely on the lower lip before slowly tilting back the bottle. She grunted with delight.

'It's like Frenching the Loire valley,' she said, passing the bottle to her companion. 'Your turn.'

As they savoured the bread and cheese they talked of sex and the arts. Ella's choice cricketer, she discovered without surprise, was a thoughtful and sensitive lover of music. He described for her in luscious terms various attempts on the part of composers to reproduce in music the sexual climax. The middle section of Strauss's *Don Juan* was blatantly orgasmic, he attested as he cracked a hot crisp radish with his cuspids. And the *Tristan* prelude was almost photographically accurate.

This led Ella to her own artistic endeavours. She wrapped one naked leg around his as she declared that ultimately the reward of all artists is sensuality, and that it is a nonsense to cramp, subvert or deny one's reward in order to deserve it. She was for taking it headlong as it came, or rooting it out.

She reached in the fly of his shorts, as if to prove her point. His cock responded to her touch, but without stiffening. She laid it in his hands like an exhausted fledging rescued by a nature lover, and reached for her camera. She shot a series of close-ups from a variety of angles. Then she posed his hands and genitals in a number of studies, culminating with one hand cupped under his balls like cuckoo eggs in a robin's nest, and the other grasping the foreskin tightly like the handlebar-grips on a bicycle. By the time she had scrutinised it through her lens from twelve inches above, below, to the side and straight-on, he had an erection she could hang her camera on.

It was time for dessert.

Ella cut herself a slice of strawberry tart and dolloped on top two scoops of thick double cream. The man sat entranced from the moment she started her miniature theatre of the sensual by licking her lips to her final curtsey when the last fragment of crust was lovingly teased inside her mouth, tumbled and fumbled between tongue and teeth, and then devoured.

'Do *you* like cream?' she asked at last.

He nodded his head furiously.

Ella swept her index finger inside the glass jar, collecting a rich glob of it.

'Then this is for you.' She stuck out her tongue and wiped the cream on to the tip of it. As the man came for his serving, she pulled her tongue back. Their lips came together and she glided into his mouth, sliding the cream from tongue to tongue, smearing it sensually around his mouth, and holding him tight until he swallowed.

Ella reached a hand behind her back to unfasten the laces of her dress. As the bodice came loose she wriggled her arms free and slid the entire dress down around her waist, over her hips, and off her legs and feet. Entirely naked, she slid her finger around the inside lip of the jar of cream a second time and smeared a blob on one of her nipples.

'Come and get your second helping,' she said, leaning back on the grass and gazing heavenwards.

He knelt beside her and licked the nearest nipple. His penis peeped patiently from his shorts, stiff-necked with curiosity. The cream rolled down the breast. He chased it around her flesh with his tongue, gobbling, and then came back to the nipple and sank his lips around it. He used both hands to cup the breast into a sharp cone and sucked as much of it into his mouth as he could. And as he sucked, his tongue still chased around the nipple, in the back of his mouth, determined not to miss the slightest trace of nourishment.

Ella gave him a third helping, on the other breast. Then she laid a trail, like mapping out a treasure hunt. She placed a tiny blob of cream at the point of cleavage between her two breasts; another in her navel; a third on the soft flesh of her abdomen under the eaves of her pubic hair; and finally, a larger dollop right on her clitoris. A tiny rivulet of cream, melted perhaps by the heat of her orgasmic detonator, trickled from there down the sweet track between her labia and pooled at the doorway of her vagina.

The man fell to his feast like a famished beast. His tongue lapped feverishly around the folds and crevices of Ella's body, his lips clamping on like limpets when they found their reward. She pushed up against him as he tried to devour her, thrilled at his passionate excitement, afraid that he would bruise her in his extravagance. He cleaned out her navel. He surfed across her abdomen. He dived into her vagina. He took all of her labia into his mouth. He tried to swallow her clitoris. She told him he was finished, but he was like a man out of his depth, grasping at her sex without looking, without listening. She tried to push his head out of her vulva with her hands. He was latched on. She bent her legs, set her naked feet on his shoulders, and pushed with all her might until he came loose.

'There's plenty,' she said reprovingly, sitting up. 'A banquet takes hours and never runs out.'

Ella cut another slice of tart and topped it with cream. 'Lie down and I'll feed you a piece properly.'

The man lay back on the grass and Ella held the tart to his mouth. He bit off a piece and ate it. Then as he swallowed, Ella held his jaw closed and smeared the rest of the tart over his mouth and chin.

'I like a close-shaved plate,' she laughed, as she picked off a large half-strawberry with her teeth and squashed it against the roof of her mouth. She squeezed another chunk of crust through his lips with her little finger and then bent down to lick a smear of cream and fruit glaze from his chin.

When the platter was empty she asked him if he liked honey and he said yes.

'Then let's share my honeypot the same way.'

She had been sitting up to the table, one knee on each side of his face just above his shoulders, her buttocks resting on his chest. Now she lifted her bottom, shifting her weight to her knees. Her top half was vertical, her honeypot inches above his face. She splayed her knees outwards slightly, bringing her cunt right down on his nose. She slid it down to his mouth. It was sticky and slippery. It was still wet with sperm from his fuck an hour or so earlier . . . his cream and Devonshire cream . . . and her honey . . . lots of her honey because she was runny with excitement now. She rubbed her cunt up over his nose and down over his chin, smearing him with cream and honey. Then she stopped over his mouth, pressing her clitoris against the end of his nose.

'Eat!' she urged him. 'Eat my cunt! Lick my honey!'

She felt his tongue slide inside her and as it spread her labia apart she felt her sticky juices oozing down. She rubbed her button against his nose as he licked her out. The she slid downwards and sank her cunt around his chin. He latched on to her clitoris with his lips and sucked as she thrust downwards. She forced her cunt against his chin so it penetrated and spread her wide and she fucked as he sucked in a sudden burst of urgency and greed. Her orgasm was steaming towards her and she cried out aloud at the speed and power of it. Then it took her breath away and she fell helplessly silent. And then it exploded through her, taking his breath too, smothering him, blasting them both with its shockwaves so that she rolled off and lay beside him, her limbs trembling on the grass until the sound returned, in deep thankful sighs, and the after-tremors gradually subsided . . . and she wrapped a leg again around him.

'Not so much a honeypot,' he said at length. 'More a bombe surprise.'

But no self-respecting banquet ends with a bang. And unlike the male member, which appreciates a pause between courses, Ella's sex stayed hot after her orgasm. The leg which was wrapped around her man strayed purposefully. She ran the instep of her foot up and down his calf from ankle to knee, curling her toes around his warm, fuzzy skin. Then she brought her thigh up to his crotch and rubbed herself against the hot poker of his erection. She swung herself up on to her knees again, this time straddling his genitals, and reached between her legs to guide his penis into her vagina. It was like lacquered wood in a silken sheath. She fucked him slowly. What came after the dessert, she asked herself. Walnuts and port? A little Stilton? Or lychees and brandy?

When the rhythm of her man's thrusting pelvis became too urgent she rolled off him. When he stabilised she knelt on all fours and invited him to come in from behind. Again he grew greedy. She crawled away from him. He learned the code of etiquette and when she stumbled into a position she particularly liked, and was threatening a selfish gluttony which would end all, *he* pulled *her* back. They relished a dozen more positions, more leisurely than athletic as time wore on. They nibbled, but voluptuously, at a dozen tasty treats. He felt that his erection, she felt that her hot ziggs, would last forever. They were both full of sex, both intoxicated with sensation.

Satiation came blissfully. He was on top of her, his chest rubbing gently against her breasts, his cock gliding smoothly in and almost out of her vagina, when she said without thinking, 'Let's *fuck*!'

He pressed in a little further, a little harder. As his pubic bone kissed hers she leaned in with her clitoris a little further, a little harder. And in a beautifully synchronised movement, the throb of her approaching orgasm tugged at his pulsing penis and the puddle of ejaculate which spurted from him pushed her ripples into drowning waves.

They lay still in each other's arms. They breathed as one. They slept, naked, under the afternoon sun of an idyllic English June.

Three dizzy hours after the start of their photographic session on the green at Pod Parva, Ella and her cricketing, music-loving assistant strolled back towards the pub. She said goodbye at the roadside, pausing for a moment to watch him cross back into the strangely sexless life of the village.

A car came between them. It stopped. There were two men inside and they wanted something. But enough was enough. Another time, perhaps, Ella thought. Then one of them jumped out, opened the back door and pushed her in. He hurried after her, pulled her arms behind her back and clamped a hand over her mouth to silence her shouts.

They were the two men from the pub . . . the ones she didn't fancy. She jerked her head round to look out of the back window as the car sped away, but her cricketer had gone.

6

ALL WELL AND GOODE

Goode took a taxi straight from Euston to his riverside apartment. It was dark inside . . . he always left the blinds down when he was away . . . And it smelled vaguely feminine and carnivorous. That was typical, too.

His ritual for shedding his country skin and stepping back into his city one was simple enough: he stripped naked, tossing his Pod Parva clothes over the back of the nearest chair, and headed for the shower. In the bathtub on The Row he vamped his way through Gilbert and Sullivan. Now he slid a Synkromeshe CD into his bathroom player and balanced the recessed speakers for a quadraphonic experience in the shower.

The soundscape of deadpan robot music and shower-hiss was barely scratched when a bleary-eyed blonde in her early twenties emerged from the master bedroom and stumbled into the breakfast-kitchen. She was wearing a pair of fluffy high-heeled mules, see-through French knickers and a skimpy sleeveless camisole with pencil-thin shoulder straps. She put a fresh filter in the coffee machine, poured herself a slug of orange juice from the fridge, and grimaced when her eye caught the time signal on the cooker. Four o'clock! She squinted round the side of a window blind, and quickly withdrew. The sun hadn't remotely thought about giving up its reign over the day.

Then she saw the pile of messy clothes. She groaned at the thought of having to share her breakfast table with a man whose presence she couldn't begin to account for. A closer scrutiny revealed brown corduroy trousers, a red chequered lumberjack shirt and a pair of hideously scuffed desert boots. She reached instinctively for an ankle-length kaftan and covered her flesh. Then she sat down and worked on her nails while she tried to remember what on earth had happened the night before.

She was on her second cup of coffee, and no wiser, when Goode came back from the shower with a towel round his waist. There was a crude, hungry look in his eyes which gave him away as the owner of the outrageous clothes. But almost naked he looked very dishy indeed, and the woman's disquiet about the events of the previous night turned to curiosity.

'Who the hell are you?' Goode asked.

'And who the hell are you, slapping around in wet bare feet as though you owned the place?'

'I do own the place.'

He sat down next to her with a controlled smile which convinced her at once of the truth of his unlikely claim. The towel fell open at the side revealing his taut, muscular thigh, and he rested his hand on her kaftan just above the knee. She gently removed it.

'Not before breakfast,' she said with the air of a someone trapped and playing for time.

'But I had breakfast eight hours ago,' Goode said. 'Like the rest of the world.' He went to the window and opened the blinds, pouring brilliant sunshine into the room.

'No! Please!' The woman sank her hungover head in her hands, hiding her eyes. When she opened them again, Goode had closed the blinds and dropped his towel. He stood three feet from her with a budding hard-on.

'So where is Sissy?' he asked, reaching down to touch one of her breasts through the silky fabric of her robe. This time she did not move it.

'So you're Liddle Georgey Bro,' she said.

'I'm George and this is Peter.' He took his penis in his other hand and stroked it once to an impressive stiffness. 'And where is darling Fuchsia?'

The woman made her acquaintance with Peter, holding him in an indifferent handshake while again playing for time with George.

'She's down at my place in the country for a few days. Mummy and Daddy are in the Med so Fuchsia went down for a spot of tennis with her friend. I rather think they didn't want company, so Fuchsia said I could use her place in town.'

'Except that it isn't her place.'

'She said you wouldn't mind. She said her little brother was very . . .'

'Accommodating?' Goode suggested, tilting his hips to slide his penis back and forth in her hand.

'Something like that.'

'And are you very accommodating?' Goode suddenly adopted an air of propriety. 'I'm sorry, I don't know your name . . .'

'Fiona.'

He began fondling the breast beneath his hand. 'Are you very accommodating, like myself, Fiona?'

She smiled with a quick blend of proper resignation and improper anticipation. 'I'm rather compromised, aren't I?'

'To be frank,' Goode said, dropping any semblance of courtesy or playfulness, 'I have just returned from a retreat involving a lengthy period of abstinence and I'm as horny as hell. I'm dying to see what you've got under that robe and I think under the circumstances you owe me a little hospitality.' He stepped back a pace, replacing her hand on his cock with his own and stroking it up and down slowly and deliberately as he watched and waited.

Fiona stood, wide awake and without a thought of breakfast. She crossed her arms in front of her, gripped the material of the kaftan at each side of her waist and bunched it up in her fingers. Slowly, she pulled it up, revealing first her shapely instep and ankles, as classic as Greek statues on pedestals in the high-heeled mules. Goode's hungry eyes tracked their way up her calves, knees and thighs to the see-through knickers whose extensive lacework revealed a pudendum entirely shaved of hair.

The kaftan swept upwards baring abdomen, navel and the bones of her lower ribs. As it covered her face, Goode's expression became ravenous. He stepped towards her, pulled one of her breasts out of the slinky camisole, and latched his mouth on it. She leaned backwards, her arms still entangled in the kaftan above her head, but Goode stifled any verbal objections by moving his mouth from her breast to her lips. He simultaneously pushed her further, with his chest against hers, until her back came to rest on the breakfast table. He searched her mouth with his tongue and as soon as she returned his kiss he held her there passionately, her arms handcuffed in the robe above her head, her mouth locked on his, and her legs dangling off the end of the table. He pushed the crotch of her knickers to one side and groped with his penis until he found the entrance to her vagina. He pushed in, pulled back; pushed in further, pulled back; and then, lubricated by her rapidly obliging juices, he plunged all the way in. Her legs came up and around him, gripping him like a vice, and his hairy pubes rubbed against the slinky silk of her knickers and the close-shaved silken skin of her font.

At precisely that moment the door opened and in came a tall girl with long dark hair, wearing a man's extra-large T-shirt for a nightie. She walked past the woman on her back on the table without looking, saying with a catty sneer, 'This is the kitchen, Fiona. It's time for breakfast, Fiona.'

But she stopped and looked at Goode. She stroked his bare thigh with the palm of her hand, gazed down admiringly at the thick shaft which was sliding in and out of her friend on the table and muttered. 'My . . . my . . .'

'No, mine!' Fiona insisted. 'He's all mine! First come first served.'

Goode eased up on his pelvic thrusts, reached for the newcomer, and pulled her close with his right arm round her waist. He latched on to her lips with his mouth, and as soon as he had engaged her tongue, slid his hand under her nightie. He eased his middle finger into her vagina and found it warm and welcoming.

Fiona, her legs still crossed behind Goode, started pumping her crotch against him. 'Hey, Melissa! He's mine! Go toast yourself a crumpet!'

Goode responded by resuming his pelvic thrusts, but he didn't let go of either set of Melissa's lips. The mindless electronic sound of the Synkromeshe orchestra made a delicious key change just as the door opened and closed again quietly, letting into the kitchen the third of sister

Fuchsia's old school chums. She was a petite girl with disproportionately large breasts which made their point impressively, even inside a pair of Goode's pyjamas.

Lallie crept up to the preoccupied threesome and pinched Goode's bottom. His hand jabbed hard up Melissa's vagina and his cock slammed roughly into Fiona.

The newcomer giggled delightedly. 'He's real!'

'Lallie!' the other two grunted, disgustedly. 'Behave yourself!'

'Behave myself?' She slid a hand between the thrusting pubes of Goode and Fiona, grabbing the base of his shaft as it emerged partway, to verify its size and vigour. 'Just like you?' She sounded bitchy, but she liked what she felt. 'Neither of you brought him home last night. So who is he? The milkman?'

Goode cut short the discussion by tearing his lips from Melissa — she didn't let them go easily — and kissing this third surprise lodger passionately on her mouth. With his left hand he took her hand off his cock, sliding all the way into Fiona again. The middle finger of his right hand was still up Melissa's vagina. Now he groped inside the fly of the striped, ill-fitting pyjamas on his left and slid his other middle finger up Lallie.

'He's our landlord,' Fiona said as she fucked him.

Lallie oohed and aahed. 'I'm hungry.'

Melissa sounded famished as she said, 'I've always fancied paying the rent on my back!'

'I found him first!' Fiona spat out, getting a stronger grip on him with her ankles crossed behind his back.

Goode was happy enough with a cunt in each hand and one on his cock, but felt he had to step in and stop them fighting.

'I'll cook an omelette big enough for everyone,' he said.

'But I want the jumbo sausage!'

Melissa grimaced. 'You always were so vulgar, Fiona.'

'I'll be cook's help,' Lallie said ingratiatingly.

Goode let go of Melissa and told her to straddle Fiona face down. She had enormously long and agile legs, one of which she swung over Fiona's crotch so she was standing in front of Goode, between him and the table, straddling his cock and the cunt which it was penetrating.

'Lie down on her,' Goode said, 'and I'll keep you both well stirred and fry you together.'

They didn't take to it naturally. Melissa leaned on her elbows, so her breasts didn't touch Fiona's. And Fiona turned her head to one side in a desperate attempt to maintain a vestige of modesty. But from where Goode stood, the long black hair of one mingled gorgeously with the blonde curls of the other, and their two cunts were perfectly served on a plate before him, one sunny side up, the other over easy.

While they struggled to maintain a little distance at the top end, in their eagerness to present their vulvas to Goode they were kissing each other at the clitoris. He pulled his cock out of Fiona and slid it back two inches higher, into Melissa. Then back again. He shoved the three longest fingers of his right hand, bunched together, into the vacant vagina and fucked them both together. Within a minute Melissa had dropped down on to Fiona and they were rubbing their breasts together, groaning mouth to cheek with pleasure, their sexual buttons firing off each other, and Goode would have sworn they couldn't have said which of them had his cock inside them at any moment.

Then Lallie climbed up on the table. Goode was using his left hand to aim and stir with his cock, his right hand to stuff the other opening. She wanted stuffing too. So she stripped and climbed up on the table, one foot either side of Melissa and Fiona, facing Goode. She only had to bend down a little to swing her enormous breasts into his face. She smothered him in her cleavage – he could do his cooking on the table blindfold by now – and then she pushed each nipple and aureola in turn into his mouth while he sucked, then both nipples together . . . She held him by the back of his head and stood on her toes, reaching up on her short athletic legs and pulling his head forward into her vulva.

This is good, Goode told himself. Good with a capital G and Goode with an e on the end. He was enjoying himself, even if he was a little uncomfortable. And it was certainly going to come as a tremendous relief.

Then Fiona said 'I want the come.'

Melissa laughed. 'He'll come where he has to.'

Goode could hardly remember which one he was in.

The two girls on the table were rushing towards their own orgasms, hair mingled together, breasts rubbing breasts, clitoris kissing clitoris . . . and even as the first wave swept outwards from their conjoined epicentre, they kept arguing about who should have his come.

Goode was spared the details. Lallie was spending at his mouth and she gripped his head tight between her upper thighs, blocking out his hearing. As he blindly swapped his hand and his cock again, in the interests of fair play, the two on the table heaved off it and then fell back into place, wrapped together, as they jerked in simultaneous orgasm, and the sudden uncontrollable motion brought him off, too, only his cock had slipped out of Melissa and fucked its last few thrusts in the crack between her and Fiona . . . between silk knickers, shaved font and jet-black bush . . . shooting its load like wild fire, into no-man's-land between the two warring crotches.

'Damn!' said Fiona.

'Shit!' said Melissa.

In that brief moment of helplessness an image of Ella Deedes flashed before Goode. She was an incorrigible flirt. She was worldly wise and daring. She was passionate and she was assertive. But above all, she was generous.

The flash brought a smile to his face.

'You're not going to kick us out then,' Lallie said.

Fiona was already back in her kaftan. 'Like hell he is. He owes us all one, by my reckoning.'

'And breakfast,' Melissa added.

Goode reckoned he was stuck with them; and if not them, others like them. This was his life in town, and once he'd turned his drawings over to his agent he would surrender himself to it. He always did. But now he had another little purpose too. However silly it was, he would do it for Ella.

He smiled again generously. 'And the best sausage goes to the one with the most helpful friend in the City.'

Soon after 'breakfast' the three girls started drinking martinis. They chatted about the clubs in town, and who were the big rollers, and whether they were heavies or sillies, and what they were driving, and who was on the passenger seat and what she was wearing. They did a modicum of washing – skin, not dishes – and a great deal of rubbing-in of various creams and ointments. They manicured and pedicured. They lacquered and rouged. And they fought tooth and nail for their turn on the telephone.

Fiona's dead cert was out of town.

Melissa got through to a cousin who owed her, but he'd never heard of SMIPT and he couldn't access his firm's database before morning.

Lallie thought she'd hit the jackpot first time. Her man told her over the phone that SMIPT Inc. came from somewhere called Pod Magna and was in the business of putting in drains. She told Fiona to open a bottle of bubbly and then grabbed hold of Goode's hand and pulled him towards the master bedroom. That was the one with the circular bed and mirrored ceiling.

But Goode wasn't satisfied. He wanted to know who owned SMIPT, where they came from and what they did. That meant names, corporate profiles, associated interests and global ambitions. He poured himself a double Scotch. And the girls went back to the phone.

By nine o'clock the dressing scene had progressed beyond body care, make-up and lingerie. Dresses were produced, tried on, discarded. Goode's advice was sought, but not especially taken. Melissa, for instance, settled on a tight mini in black PVC.

'I'm not keen on the sheen,' Goode volunteered.

Melissa shrugged her shoulders. 'I don't have much choice. It's the only thing I've got that wipes off without leaving a stain.'

Lallie explained: 'She's dating a stockbroker on your behalf. But Quickie Dickie won't hand over the goods until he's had his pound of flesh.'

Melissa smiled at Goode. 'It's OK, it won't take long. He likes it in lifts.'

'And what if he's just playing you for a ride?'

Lallie said 'Then it's my turn to take on Baby James. He says he'll tell you all you want to know once I've tucked him in properly. It's a cinch.'

'And if *he* doesn't behave himself,' Fiona said, with the flourish and certainty of a paramour at full back, '*I've* got a date with Toni.'

Goode hardly dared ask. 'Tony?'

'She's got the loosest tongue in the City. But you've got to humour her. She'll only share what she wants where she wants and when she wants.'

'It sounds like it's going to be a busy night.' He clapped his hands twice. 'When do we start?'

Fiona insisted they hire a cab for the night and start with a steak. 'If I'm going to have to trail round after you lot all hours I need a trusty steed and some cowboy food in my belly.'

They drank beer with their steer in a Yankee place off the Strand, but after that Melissa said she needed a real drink so they drifted up into Soho. They hopped from one bar to another, showing off Goode, who was playing quiet, and discovering to their surprise that he had made noises on this route before. They stumbled on a private party with an ace sax combo, upstairs at Zedekiah's, and Goode danced with them all in turn. Lallie and Melissa grumbled because Fiona got the slow shuffler.

When it was time for Melissa's date they all piled into their cab and trekked back along the Strand, up Ludgate Hill and into the City. The Richard in question patronised what he called 'the working man's club' in the penthouse of an office block. He carried a phone with him everywhere, and tracked the markets continuously, from the close on Wall Street on through the night to Tokyo, Seoul and Singapore. He worked fast. His attention was total, but only lasted for seconds. Then it was the next client, the next deal. The risks were big but they were calculated, and he played them stone cold.

'I won't be long,' Melissa said as she left the others in the lobby. They stood outside the lift and watched her progress to the top floor.

'He can't spare the time to lie down,' Fiona told Goode. 'He doesn't even have time to put it in. A bit of a frott in the lift and he can get straight back to his phone.'

'Isn't it a bit risky?' Goode asked.

'There's only offices on the other floors, and they've long gone home.'

'But at the bottom?'

'Gives him a goal, doesn't it? He watches the numbers as they go down.'

Fiona lit a cigarette. 'Here they come.'

The down arrow above the door on the ground floor lit up. Ella's information was galloping towards them and Fiona described its progress like a racing commentary.

'The doors have closed and they're away! "I'm all yours," she says. "What are you waiting for?" And she flashes her arse at him.'

The illuminated number eight went out and seven came on.

'He's got his thing out already . . . doesn't want to stain his own pants. She's pouting her lips at him. He moves in on her.'

The seven went, six lit up.

'He puts one hand on her tit, the other on her arse . . . he pushes her into the corner . . . he presses his thing against her fanny, against the plastic . . . no time for flesh . . .'

Five lit up.

'He's pressing hard. It's uncomfortable but she looks at the numbers, not long to go . . . He humps her through her clothes . . .'

Four.

'He's squashing her . . . belly to belly . . . his prick in the middle . . . Then suddenly he steps back . . .'

Three.

'His jism squirts over her skirt . . . it's fast and big, like everything he does . . . it dribbles off the PVC and splashes on the floor.'

Two.

'He shakes the last glob off the end of his prick and stuffs it back in his pants . . . zips up . . . She's got a tissue out for the skirt . . .'

One.

He checks that his tie is straight . . . runs both hands through his hair to smooth it down . . . coughs once to clear his throat, and steps right up to the door.'

The lift bobbed to a halt at ground level and the doors opened. Quickie Dickie stepped out without a backwards glance and walked straight past Goode and the two girls without looking. He told the doorman where he could be contacted and hurried to his waiting car, where he took an urgent call from Sydney.

Goode offered his hand to Melissa. She seemed to him untouched: calm and collected, with not the slightest hint of blush or flush. But she stepped carefully over what was undoubtedly a large splatter of sperm on the floor of the lift.

She handed him a piece of paper with a smile of triumph. It was typed and unsigned, on paper with no address or letterhead; 'SMIPT is a paper company not involved in any competitive trading or manufacture. Title-holder for property in heart of England, chiefly a vulgar country house with pretensions attractive to Americans. Wholly owned by a wealthy oversexed Texan called Blas Carnel.'

Lallie read over Goode's shoulder. Then she said, 'I bet Baby James can do better than that.'

So they rode their taxi round to James's firm. James was even more obsessive about his work than Richard. James worked so fast and hard and long, he even slept in his office . . . usually in a reclining chair in reach of his phone and his fax and his VDU. But every once in a while he treated himself to a proper nap in a real cot, which he kept in a little filing room off his main office. And he liked a nice buxom nanny to tuck him in.

This time Fiona ran the commentary as they waited outside for Lallie.

' "Let's get you ready for bed then," she says as soon as he puts the phone down. He smiles and looks obedient, but never says a word. She takes him by the hand and leads him into the back room . . . She's closing the door now, as he lies down on a low couch . . . She's unfastening her blouse . . . She slides her hand up inside the back of her blouse and unhooks her bra. She pulls it down off her shoulders and lets out her tits. He reaches for one with his hand, and plays with the nipple . . . Then she leans over him and he takes the other one in his mouth. He sucks the nipple, then its crinkly brown halo, then as much of the tit as he can get.'

Melissa produced a silver hip flask from her bag and passed it round.

'But she won't waste time.' Fiona went on. 'She'll have unfastened his belt by now, and unzipped his fly . . . She'll be pulling his trousers down, then his underpants. His prick's half awake, swollen but not stiff. She'll say something like "There's a good boy. This won't take a minute." Then she'll open a drawer next to the cot, whip out a nappy, and slide it under him.'

Goode nearly choked on the Southern Comfort. He splattered and coughed and passed the flask on. 'I need some fresh air.'

'Won't be long now,' Fiona said. 'She's got the pins in. He's sucking his thumb. But he's being a naughty boy. Nanny waits until he's finished and then slides her hand in to check. Yes, he's a very naughty boy indeed, wetting a brand-new nappy. She tells him so as she unfastens the pins. She slides the nappy out. She dries him with handy wipes. Then she sprinkles on some baby powder. Now he looks happy. He's well and truly rested. Restored and ready to rejoin the fray. She pats the powder round his little willie and then pulls up his underpants . . . then his trousers . . .'

Goode dimly heard a telephone ringing, inside the office.

Fiona said, 'Then the phone rings so he sits up and sees to his fly and his belt himself. Nanny is trying to get her bra back on. They hustle back into the office. He answers the phone and passes her a sheet of paper. She says thanks and makes for the door. He's talking to a finance minister in Brasilia, or a banker in New York, but he tips her a wink as she leaves.'

The door opened and Lallie came out. She passed the note straight to Goode. It was dusted with scented talcum powder and made him sneeze.

But Baby James was not much more informative than Quickie Dickie. He listed the Carnel chap as very wealthy, not just plain wealthy, and instead of oversexed he called him a poseur. He gave his address as Pod Castle, which rather made his point.

Goode had had enough. Ella Deedes and her colourful imagination were a world away and he wanted to forget about them both. He screwed up the paper.

Lallie's face crumpled with disappointment. But more to the point, Fiona now insisted it was her turn to earn the rights to the big sausage.

Goode tried to get out of the date with her stockbroker. 'I'll devote the rest of the night to your pleasure,' he said. Male stockbrokers were one thing: he couldn't begin to contemplate the pressures on the infinitely rarer female of the species . . . or the particularities of their sexual-energy safety valves. 'We'll pick up some champagne and I'll give all three of you the time of your lives,' he promised desperately.

But the competitive urge was strong in Fiona, and she wouldn't give in. They drove to a late-night bar in Chelsea for her appointment with Toni, and Fiona insisted that Goode stay with her. She wasn't taking any chances on him slipping away. That meant Lallie and Melissa stayed too. They escorted him one on each arm and one two paces behind. Like military police, Goode thought.

Against all expectations, or perhaps in part because of them, Toni appeared like a liberating angel. She was sitting by herself at a corner table and smiled beautifully, simply, gracefully, generously – 'I think I'm falling in love,' Goode whispered to himself – as soon as she saw them approach.

She greeted them all and Goode ordered drinks. Lallie started reliving the snubs and counter-snubs of Ascot. Melissa bitched about her intrigues with the centre-court coterie at Wimbledon. And Toni smiled pleasantly, taking an interest but without being drawn into the nastiness, deflecting the snide remarks and coming back with some straightforward news of her own about the theatre or a new French film she had seen. Goode relaxed. He forgot all about his mission for Ella Deedes and his promise of prize sex to his three lodgers. As he watched the tantalising feminine gestures of the delightful Toni – the way she kept flicking back her short, shag-cut hair, making her metallic earrings shimmer, and flashed her teeth like jewels – he started thinking of sex for himself. This woman was sweet and sexy, oozing the promise of pleasure, but there was something strangely enigmatic about her that he couldn't put his finger on. It made the prospect of sex extra exciting.

A few couples were bopping unenergetically to a disco opposite the bar, and Fiona asked Toni for a dance. Fair enough, Goode thought. It was her date, after all, and it gave him a chance to look at the rest of the body of the angel he was falling in love with.

She was wearing a short, tight skirt, sheer black nylons with seams running up the back, and black shoes with four-inch heels. The heels made her tall – she was tall already – but she walked on them easily, and danced naturally, as though the shoes were a favoured extension of her long, lithe legs. She was like one of those strong, leggy models from the sixties, before the emaciated look came in.

She smiled like a model, too. When she came back to the table, Goode patted her upper thigh and told her she walked like a photograph and danced like a spirit of the air. He was hot for her body, and she loved him for it. She leaned towards him imperceptibly and whispered in his ear.

'Blas Carnel is the man you want. He's from Texas and he's big in communications. I mean really big.'

Goode couldn't give a damn about Blas Carnel any more, but he'd listen to anything this voice wanted to say. It was even sexier for its secretiveness. And the enigma was there in the voice, too. It was sweet with favours and yet spiced with just a hint of huskiness.

Goode's hand, still resting on her thigh, began to stroke the sleek nylon of her stockings, hidden from the view of the others by the table. Toni obviously liked the attention, and whispered again, with an air of rewarding him:

'There's something very big coming in telecommunications. Carnel doesn't want it to break until he's tied up the big money. But if it works, it's going to take advertising somewhere totally new. New and big risk.'

Goode listened without hearing. He would have listened to her reading from the telephone directory. As she spoke he slid his hand up her skirt. He felt the stocking top . . . the elastic strap which fastened the stocking to the belt around her abdomen . . . the tender flesh of her inner, upper thigh. Then she casually took his wrist in her hand and pushed his hand down. Again she smiled.

Fiona suggested a move. She was jealous, Goode thought, but he didn't care. Toni wanted to try a new place in Soho and he was content enough watching those gorgeous legs manoeuvring in and out of the cab. Sitting next to her, he was intoxicated by the scent of her body and perfume. Climbing the stairs to the club he dropped back a pace or two to watch her walk and it gave him a hard-on. And she soaked up his admiration like royalty.

The three lodgers were getting steadily plastered and bitched away at each other and their peers more and more lewdly as the night wore on. They ordered pink champagne and Lallie danced with the ice bucket, hugging it to her huge and barely covered breasts. Toni drank Irish coffee.

'There's a rumour he's found a new way of giving consumer products sex appeal,' she told Goode, flicking her hair back and wetting her lips.

He said, 'I want to kiss the nape of your neck.'

She bent forward slightly, and without cringing offered him the soft place just below her hairline. As he touched his lips to it she said, 'I don't mean psychologically, I mean tangibly.'

He hadn't a clue what she was talking about. He kissed behind her ear. But then she pulled away, gently.

'I mean he's planning to transmit television adverts simultaneously with a tangible sexual energy, and it's going to be worth billions.'

Goode was ready for a bit of tangible sexual transmission himself. 'Will you come back to my place?' he asked.

She shook her head with a sense of wistful resignation. It was nearly three in the morning. 'I have to be at the office in a few hours,' she said. 'And I have to bathe and change.'

'Tomorrow, then. What time can I see you after work?'

'We'll see,' she said, with an indifference which jolted him. 'Things sometimes look different in the bright light of day.' But she took pity on him when she saw how far his face fell, and added encouragingly, 'You can drive me home. We could take the long way round.'

Goode tried to pack his three lodgers off in another cab, but they weren't having it and to his surprise Toni took their side. She said they should all stick together to the end, they made such a good team.

In the taxi Toni sat Goode in the middle with Melissa on one side and Lallie on the other, herself and Fiona taking the dickey seats facing backwards. Goode was too confused to complain. She gave the driver their destination and the time she wanted to arrive, and then pulled down the blind to give them privacy.

Melissa promptly kissed Goode on the mouth, thrusting her tongue inside him with pent-up lust. He felt a warm hand slide inside his shirt and caress his chest. Other hands were unfastening his trousers and stroking his inner thigh. As they moved with something like an air of purpose through the streets he could hear the intermittent noise of early-morning London, and feel the warmth of its street lights as they gave the cab their undivided attention. He slumped back on the seat and relaxed.

Then Toni said, 'Now girls, watch how it's done properly.'

Melissa and Lallie withdrew their attention and when Goode opened his eyes he found all four women concentrating avidly on his exposed and very erect penis. Toni was kneeling on her wrap at his feet. Over her shoulder he could see the tan leather soles and long black spikes of her high-heeled shoes, the gentle curve of her calves, the fabric of her tiny skirt stretched tight over her buttocks. Blood coursed through his hot veins and he felt his cock lurch even bigger. The small space in the back of the cab was electric with sexual energy. The others were only watching, perhaps, but he knew they were enjoying themselves intensely. Blood was coursing too in the dark, untouched folds of their knickers. Labia were engorged. All the tender places were flushed with excitement.

Toni liked them all watching. Just as she had relished their attention all evening, so she wanted to be watched now. She was as flushed as any of them.

Goode decided to watch too. He would watch and be watched, and enjoy showing them what happened when it was 'done properly'.

Toni held the loose folds of foreskin just below the glans of his cock precisely between her thumb and forefinger. She squeezed gently. She twisted the skin sideways, like a miniature Chinese burn. Then she rubbed it up and down over the corona, the rim of the glans, slowly concealing and then revealing the bright red head.

As he watched her hands at work, Goode felt her tongue. With the tip flexed hard, she traced around the latticework of his tight scrotum, up the crease of his thigh on one side, and down the other. She probed behind his balls, stretching the length of her tongue beneath him, along his perineum towards his anus.

She gripped the shaft of his cock half way up with her left hand and squeezed, cupping her right hand over the top of his glans and twisting as if she were juicing a lemon . . . clockwise and then anticlockwise . . . as the tip of her tongue probed meticulously, pressed, ran over his lower sex in tiny wet circles. She knew just the place, just the pressure. He gave no signals and made no movement himself. But uncannily, as if he willed her, as if she knew exactly what it felt like for him, and what he wanted next, she led him along his private clifftop path with its breathtaking vistas.

Then Toni slid a hand under his balls, cupping them, and ran the tip of her tongue, pressing hard, along the spongy length of engorged tissue which was like the seam of his cock. As she reached the tip of it he almost dived off his cliff. He balanced precariously. He watched closely as she pursed her lips into a rosebud and brought it down on his head, making a hard, slow penetration. She took him in further than he dreamed possible – he must be halfway down her throat, gagging her – and then slowly she withdrew, leaving him drenched in her saliva.

She resumed with the tip of her tongue, tracing the length of him, swirling round the glans, and then sinking her lips around the head. She held his foreskin between pursed lips and rotated it; she gripped and started a rhythmic up and down. He tripped then. Sitting motionless, helpless on the seat of the cab, he knew he had plunged from his cliff. He was in free fall. Toni knew it too, and treated him to some stunning acrobatics before he struck water. She made a ring round the base of his shaft with the fingers of one hand and frigged him with it while her other hand probed and delved ever deeper beyond his balls. Her lips moved swiftly and surely up and down the top half of his shaft, synchronised perfectly with the fingers below; and deep inside her mouth, her tongue frisked the head of him. At precisely the same moment they both glimpsed the end of free fall as the water raced up to meet them. Toni pulled her mouth two inches from him, and Goode watched the first squirt of his sperm dive from the tiny hole at the tip of his cock and splash on to her tongue. Quickly she enveloped him again, the second pulse throbbing out against the back of her throat. She swallowed fast and gripped him again with her lips; sucked hard and fast; and drew out his spasm, pulling him down to the very ocean floor, sprawling, spent, in a fluid, breathless ecstasy.

She gently frigged him and sucked to drain away the very last of his come, swallowing slowly and more casually now, in tandem with his carefree spaciness.

Goode closed his eyes at last. He felt loving hands tucking him away, zipping him up. Then the cab came to a halt. Toni was scrambling off her knees . . . she opened the door . . . she was leaving!

Goode reached for her hand to pull her back. 'Can't I at least repay the compliment?'

'It would take too long,' Fiona said, relapsing into her catty tone of voice as the cab pulled away. 'She's so particular about dressing. Getting her cock out is like unwrapping an Egyptian mummy . . .'

7

APPLIED MECHANICS

The car in which Eleanor Deedes had been abducted sped directly to Pod Manor. Within minutes it pulled off the road, halted briefly for the security guard at the gate in the perimeter wall and then crunched its way up the gravel driveway between dense, gloomy laurels.

Ella felt a sense of foreboding. The two gangsters who had pulled her off the streets kept up a pretence that she had been invited to an important business meeting. But it felt to her remarkably like being kidnapped.

She was taken through a side door and up a flight of stairs. The place looked sterile and smelled like an institution.

'Mr Carnel has arranged for dinner in an hour.'

'I'm not hungry.'

They pushed her through a door into a spartan bedroom. As if they'd removed anything you might use to harm yourself, she thought. Or harm them.

One of the heavies nodded towards another door on the far side. 'There's a bathroom through there.' He spoke with an air of threatening courtesy. 'You'll want to freshen up for dinner.'

And then they left her.

She heard a key turn in the lock and resisted the urge to run after them, to rattle the door and scream at them. The window was locked shut too. And there was no telephone. She would compose herself. She would stay calm. She would prepare herself to seize the right opportunity to escape when it presented itself. A bath wasn't such a bad idea after all.

Ella filled the tub deep and hot, and let the water caress

and console her. She soaked away the memory of her delightful lunch on the green and prepared herself for dinner in the castle. Then she dried herself on the single rather mean towel and stepped gratefully from the linoleum of the bathroom back on to the bedroom carpet.

She noticed at once that her clothes had gone. She hurried to the door and tried it. Still locked. Someone had stolen in while she was in the bath and taken her clothes. She cast around desperately. The small towel was soaking wet and would hardly cover her. There was a wardrobe but it too looked mean and unhelpful. She opened it with trepidation.

And then she laughed.

At one end of the wardrobe there was an Annie Oakley cowgirl outfit; at the other, an Indian squaw costume.

Ella Deedes had never much liked playing cowboys and Indians. But she liked the feel of leather and suede against her skin and decided she was going to enjoy dressing up. She chose freely from the two sets of clothing, mostly on the basis of sensuality, and felt that in doing so she reclaimed at least a token of her freedom of action.

She jumped when a voice coming through a small speaker she had not noticed told her to proceed to the dining room across the hallway. She tried the door and found it unlocked.

The landing was deserted. There was not the slightest sound of human activity. But inside the room opposite she found a table set for two, laden with food and emanating some delicious odours. The sprung door clicked behind her. Clicked and locked.

'So where's Buffalo Bill?' she asked aloud. 'Or is it George Armstrong Custer?'

A voice answered through an intercom. The speaker was above a broad mirrored section on the far wall and Ella presumed correctly that she was being observed by her host through one-way glass.

'I shall be eating with you, Ms Deedes, but until we have come to some understanding and I am satisfied that my current business activity is safe from your further interference, I must take the precaution of isolating myself and my associates from a certain energy you seem to possess in unnatural abundance.'

Ella listened carefully to the quality of the voice. This man was an operator, she thought. Sex and power. Sex and money. Sex and greed. She didn't like the sound at all.

'I see you found something to wear. Your own clothes were stained with . . . should we say . . . a wide assortment of juices?'

Ella shrugged her shoulders.

'Park your goddamn ass, honey, and let's start on the soup.'

She lifted the lid of a silver tureen and served herself the lobster bisque which it contained. And he's a wanker, she told herself.

Behind the glass Blas Carnel slurped his soup and dribbled down his chin. His personal squaw, who was now naked, dabbed him clean with a napkin. Then Carnel signalled for her to get out his cock. He was going to enjoy his *diner à deux*. 'Hell and tarnation, but she's dangerous,' he mumbled as the squaw started stroking his stiff cock up and down and he scrutinised his captive.

Ella had torn the long sleeves off the Indian tunic at the shoulder seams and was wearing them as tight leggings. She had tied them round her mid-thigh using strands of beads from the Indian necklace, and the elbow fringes danced delectably over her calves when she moved her legs. The tougher leather of the cow-girl mini-skirt left a ring of about two inches of naked flesh at the top of the leggings, and the ankle boots with heels and spurs gave her feet a decisiveness which almost ended Carnel's meal before the main course.

'Slow down, honey,' he whispered. 'This girl's dynamite!'

The naked squaw held her hand motionless round his cock just long enough for him to regain control, and then resumed her steady up-and-down stroke at a slower speed. 'What will happen to her?' she asked with apparent detachment.

'I shall get from her what I want, and when the experiment is over she will never have another sexual thought in her pretty little life. I'll have her dropped in the Australian outback or someplace, where she can be a schoolteacher or a missionary.' He smiled cruelly at the fate worse than death.

Ella's long naked arms pushed her empty soupbowl away and poured a glass of beer from the pitcher before her. The ragged edges of the suede shift round her shoulders created a tantalising ambiguity. She looked rugged and muscular . . . she looked like a rifled package . . .

His squaw poured him a beer.

Ella had given her Indian top some shape by pinning two sheriff's badges from the Annie Oakley shirt right over the nipples of her breasts. And she had used the rest of the bead necklace to tie up her thick golden hair into a wild Mohican shock. She looked like a goddess of fertility.

'So you need to protect yourself from me?' Ella asked. She heaped a serving of delta rice and chicken gumbo on to her plate, leaned back on two legs of her chair and crossed her legs at the ankle with her boots up on the edge of the table.

Dead right he did. That line of pressed flesh running almost to her crotch . . . she was facing the mirror on purpose, and she felt sure she could hear him breathing heavily.

He answered her combatively, through the intercom. 'I've drained this village, and I'm going to drain you too, honey.'

Big clever dick, she thought. She bet he was the type that knew just how long he was. But if he couldn't show off his big dick, he *could* show off how clever he was. She told him she was sure he was very smart.

'You'll be my first guinea pig on the individual machine, sugar. And it's going to be a dream.' He tucked into his own gumbo.

Ella liked only her own dreams; she always found other people's boring. So she asked him how he drained the village, and sure enough, he was eager to show off his cleverness.

'How did I do it? I constructed a gigantic orgone box. I turned an English village green into one hell of an orgone box! You see baby, Wilhelm Reich was right years ago. You've heard of him, I can tell. Nutcase. He said to alternate layers of organic and inorganic materials to focus the orgone energy. But he didn't have the technology. It takes thousands of microscopic layers. It takes silicon chip technology. And when you reach the right number there's a quantum leap in effectiveness. You don't just get a smoothing-out like he wanted for his so-called therapy. You get a massive condensation that can drain an entire village of its sexual energy!'

He had to stop because he was working himself up into a state of dangerous excitement again. Squaw took her hand right off his cock to let it cool down and carefully wiped the spicy creole sauce from his chin with a napkin.

'So the weird pipes I saw really do drain, even though they're solid.' Ella was about to ask him where they drained the sexuality to and what he did with the energy, once he'd got it. But it suddenly occurred to her that if he told her too much she might become a liability that he would have to drain off far more than her sex drive. Did she know too much already? Would he have to drain her to extinction? She pushed her plate away and took her feet off the table. She sat demurely and cut herself a dainty slice of Jefferson Davis pie.

'There's lemon sauce for the pie, honey,' Carnel said with a lewd sneer.

Maybe he got off on the alluring victim look. She sat up and tried to look businesslike and boring. When the villain caught the good guy he explained all his tricks to show how smart he was and then he launched into his justification to show that he wasn't actually such a bad sort after all. That would be his apologia and it would mean he was purging himself for the sin he was about to commit. She swamped her pie in the thin acid sauce and hoped for the best.

'Pod Whatsit's a safe sort of place now, right honey? Before you came along and stirred it up anyways. Nobody using their sex to get what they shouldn't have. No grabbing it and hiding it, or flaunting it and playing tricks. Now if I can clean a place up, take away all the unfair sex that's based on individuals and personality and give it back equally, to the community, in a way that's fair, that you can measure out on a reasonable basis, that you can acquire with something like tokens – like money for instance – then that's got to be a more humane way. You're goddamn right it has. That's where you can start having something like *real* sexual equality, like in the Constitution, cash up front . . .'

But Ella couldn't hear him properly. There was something about the lemon sauce. It tasted astringent. Her tongue went fuzzy. And she was suddenly exhausted. She couldn't keep her eyes open. She felt herself slumping forward and twisted sideways to avoid falling in the food. There was something terribly wrong with the lemon sauce. She must know too much. This was it. Her chair tippled over and she fell on the floor in a crumpled heap and lay still.

The naked squaw had been watching Ella intently and subconsciously increased the tempo of her hand on Carnel's cock. He too, was distracted by the prostrate body, wondering if it might be safe for him to go in and have his way with her. His cock took the decision out of his hand and he took his cock out of the squaw's hand, holding her head down so that he could come in her mouth while getting on with his pie and making no mess.

When Ella came round from the drugged dessert she felt stretched in the body and taut in the limbs. She emerged from an exciting dream which had the effect of focusing her attention, as she regained consciousness, less on her aching head and more on her breasts and vulva, which were thoroughly exposed and seemed to be enjoying an independent wakefulness.

She was standing with her feet apart and her arms stretched out above her head, so her limbs formed a narrow sideways cross. And yet the standing was effortless. Her wrists and ankles were held in place by soft but unmoveable straps. And round her waist and hips there was a sort of vice, fur lined but firm, supporting her and at the same time making it impossible for her to move. She couldn't see a thing. But she could feel touch at certain points – like her nipples, her armpits and behind her ears . . .

She presumed she was still dreaming, though all her sensations seemed awake.

A dim light, as though on a screen in front of her, gradually grew brighter. And she heard gentle tones of New Age music which swirled into something more substantial with rippling flute trills and resonant pan pipes. It was all rather relaxed and sensual. There was a scent of musk in the air, its heady fragrance mixed with the slightest undertow of smegma, the acrid herald of stiff cock.

Dream on, she thought with a sweet smile.

The light on the screen grew into a psychedelic swirl of coloured fluids which moved voluptuously in time with the music. Then they began to assume phallic shape. They played with each other lustfully. It was extremely clever. It was also undeniably erotic. A tiny shiver of awareness murmured through her body from one erogenous zone to the next. And in each hot spot, again she felt the sensation of touch. She forced her eye from the compulsive copulating shapes on screen and looked down at her breast. Little round stickers were fastened there, with wires attached, like tiny electrodes. There were more under her arms. She couldn't move enough to see her crotch. So she followed one of the wires, from her left nipple. It lead to a sort of machine on wheels. A robot! Where did she dream up this stuff? A sexy robot, no doubt about it . . . she could smell his stiffy! And he was coming towards her! His enormous phallus was aimed right at her pussy! She could sense it homing in. And boy was she ready. She would take it all! She wanted to be stuffed! She was tied up, captive, defenceless, and she was going to take this huge robotic dildo and fuck!

Her expectations were suddenly shattered by the cold sneering voice of Blas Carnel. 'Just taking a little smear, honey, to give a reading of vaginal lubrication.' And she realised with a shock that this was no dream.

She pulled and tugged at her bonds, but there was no give. For a moment she despaired. She closed her eyes and mentally kicked herself for getting into this absurd and dangerous situation. Then she remembered Goode. George Goode was in London, busily running down her leads. He was on the case! And he was conscientious, smart, even heroic perhaps, given the chance. The role of damsel in distress, she told herself, always came with a knight in shining armour.

At precisely that moment the real George Goode, sated with his experience of Quickie Dickie, Baby James and Pantie-Queen Toni was obliterating all thought of SMIPT and looking forward to a luscious restorative session with his three lodgers. And Ella was depending on him, and him alone, to save her life.

The amorphous erotic shapes on the screen began to take on human attributes. Soon she was watching a soft-focus, close-up liaison between an anonymous penis and an anonymous vulva. She was aware that the instrument probing her own vagina would get a positive reading on lubrication, even an excessive reading. She just had to hold out until Goode reached her.

The probe retracted, and then returned in another guise. This time it was humming. She could hear it over the sound of synthesised harp and krummhorn. And instead of going straight inside her, it played around her labia and clitoris, vibrating with a delicious and tireless intensity. The other points of contact, in all her erogenous zones, also seemed to change their function. Instead of, or as well as, measuring her state of arousal, they now acted as stimuli. It wasn't exactly heat, or pressure, or electricity, or alpha waves or beta waves; it was a little shot of pure sexual energy. That was the only conclusion she could come to. It was like a dozen little catalysts, speeding up her reactions, a dozen tiny detonators, and she felt a moment of panic: that she would be powerless to resist and that somehow this maniac really had found a way to drain a person of their sex. When Goode rescued her it would be too late. She would have to return with him to sexless Pod Parva – Little Dick – and spend the rest of her life bird-watching.

The robot played more adventurously with his vibrator, running it down her inside thigh at a ticklish high frequency. She almost cried at the tease of it. 'Georgey Porgey pudding and pie,' she said to herself. 'Kissed the girls and made them cry.'

And there lay her salvation. She finished the rhyme: 'When the girls came out to play, Georgey Porgey ran away'.

She had been cornered by a wanker and a bully, but she wasn't going to cry! She would teach him not to underestimate her will and capacity for sex!

'Come on, Georgey Porgey,' she said aloud, 'Let's play!'

The vibrator accelerated to ultra-high frequency and hovered around her clitoris, marking out little circles with its tip. But Georgey had another hand, with another throbbing mechanical stiffy, and this one slid deep inside her vagina, vibrating profoundly. Ella was playing goalie against two at once, a fast dribbler and a powerful long shot, and soon she was in a welcome sweat. All her concentration was in her crotch. Clitoris and cunt . . . clitoris and cunt . . . It was a brilliant ploy. She deflected one shot and then another until she could move no faster. They came at her together and she tripped into her orgasm.

Ella's crotch convulsed and Georgey withdrew his probes. But her writhing was constrained by the vice around her hips. Denied their natural route, the waves of her climax were reflected inwards. They coursed up and down the length of her body, into her limbs, which jerked involuntarily in their bonds. But there was no give. She weakened. She wanted to collapse. But she was held firmly. The echo of her orgasm came back to the centre again, and her abdomen pulsed, her crotch seemed to glow.

The wanker must have been watching. 'One down . . .' he said over the intercom, like a commentator at a steeplechase.

I'll have you too, Ella thought. I'll last you out! She ran her tongue over her lips in anticipation. She was still hot. She could trip half a dozen times on this same high!

Now three videos were showing at once, one straight in front of her and one to each side. The view had expanded, from genitals to whole bodies: naked bodies, making love in pairs. It was the missionary position on screen one, doggy-style on screen two and standing face-to-face on screen three. But where was Georgey? She wanted to beat the man on screen one and he was very close . . .

Then she felt a cold metal hand slide between her legs from behind. Sly Georgey! He'd crept up behind her! Three self-lubricating robotic fingers slid between her bottom cheeks and up her vagina while one rubbed slowly around and over her clitoris. Go, go go! She beat the man on the screen by a hairsbreadth! Well done Georgey!

The soundtrack had become an unobtrusive mix of sitar and tabla, with a voice-over which said solemnly, 'Two down . . .'

Couple One were replaced by a more adventurous pair, with the man sitting and the woman kneeling over him, face to face. Ella gasped at the prospect of witnessing the entire Kāma Sūtra. But the woman on screen three was getting somewhere and Ella rushed along to keep her company. Georgey was still at it . . . Ella shuddered and tripped.

'Three down . . .'

On screen two the couple were pacing each other. They were going to come together. And their pause for synchronisation just gave Ella time to catch up herself. Georgey increased his tempo and pressure as if he could sense the need. Maybe he was getting feedback from his sensors in her sundry hot spots.

'Four down . . .'

Then came a superb double act. On screen two, a couple in the classic 69 position; on screen three another couple sucking each other, but the nine was inside out! The man lay on his back on the ground and the woman stood above his head, facing away from his cock. She bent over backwards like a limbo dancer, bending at the knees to bring her crotch down to the man's tongue and tilting her head way over to take his cock in her mouth. Ella writhed inwardly at the sheer grace and muscle of the movement and as soon as the cock slithered into the woman's mouth, she came for the fifth time on this one rush.

The man watching from outside missed his count. Maybe he'd been distracted. Maybe he'd come himself! Let's see him rapid fire five times in a row on the same big shoot, Ella thought. But she had slumped at last herself. And Georgey had withdrawn.

Ella breathed deeply as the music changed to a kaleidoscopic Mahler symphony: dramatic, romantic, self-centred, crude, graceful, indulgent, all-encompassing . . . And the kinemascope launched a new programme.

On the centre screen, a couple in evening dress; on the right, in motorbike gear; on the left, in jogging outfits. Three slow strips. Denim jackets, silk shirts, knee-length boots . . . white ankle socks and black nylons . . . french knickers, G-strings, gunmetal medallions . . . she watched them all come off. The man on the left held the woman's naked feet together and fucked the gap formed by the insteps with his cock. The woman on the right was doing aerobics over the prostrate body of her mate. And centre screen the woman was hunched face down over a pile of cushions while her man spread her cheeks and enjoyed a *feuille de rose*. Ella dipped into each scene like best man at a wedding buffet. Soon the man on the left had swapped feet for breasts, woman right was doing press ups and woman centre had her man face down and was rimming him.

The machine took her by surprise again. It had crept silently alongside and came at her from both sides at once. But this time instead of rigid vibrators, its digits came like sculptured dildos. They were warm, oily and pliant. Fatso probed and penetrated her vagina. The slender one slid its way between her bottom cheeks and into her tighter aperture. They nestled, still. Ella rocked. Her freedom of movement was measured in millimetres, but the freedom of her climax in kilometres, leagues, versts, infinities! It was an earth-mover, and the movement wouldn't stop. She went on rocking with her infinitely potent, infinitesimal movement. And she watched.

On one screen there was a man in a business suit and a woman dressed like a circus ringmaster, in tall boots, coattails and top hat. She swished a long whip. Ella turned her head. A woman in a French maid's outfit touched her toes and her master's hand came down in a playful smack on her bottom. On the other side, a young nurse was strapping her patient down on his bed. The businessman had pulled down his trousers and the ringmistress was cracking her whip and coming ever closer. The maid was on her hands and knees, the cane handle of her feather duster in the hands of her master; the patient was naked and nurse was probing his defenceless body with her stethoscope. The wedding buffet catered for both sides of the family, and friends from all walks of life. Ella came with delight for the second time on this high.

The scenes climaxed too, and were followed by others. There were two boys in the Navy, alone in the steamy engine room . . . a dominatrix with a male slave at her feet . . . a pair of lesbian mud wrestlers . . .

Few of the dishes were original, and not all were to Ella's taste, but she couldn't help but be impressed by the scale of the entertainment. She came a third time out of sheer sympathetic exuberance.

She watched water sports and dungeon lore. She rocked her way through gay sex. She watched black men fuck white women and oriental men fucked by black women. She climaxed six times in close succession before Georgey Porgey withdrew his favours and she slunk again in her bonds, reflecting for the first time that it would be very pleasant now to rest on her laurels.

Georgey had a different notion. He came back at her with vibrating pads: one held over her mons, so that she could lean against it with her clitoris, and the other sweeping her *derrière*. It gave her a constant sensual massage, interspersed with more acute movements which felt like getting a light spanking with a hairbrush.

She came three times in that sequence, while watching group sex scenes in threes and fours. They were beautifully choreographed; some all male, some all female, and others mixed. She thought the soundtrack was Vivaldi.

It seemed to go on for hours, one huge multiple orgasm after another. Was she getting sore? Was she getting tired? Was she getting *drained*?

There was a series of grand orgies, from bath-house scale to opera-house, music courtesy of Mozart. Ella came twice.

There was a set built around popular fantasies, with lush art and science teachers demonstrating the procreative act for the benefit of the sixth-form biology class, and the entire football team fucking the guest of honour as they filed past, in front of a crowd of thousands. Ella mirrored almost every climax with one of her own.

Behind his one-way glass, Blas Carnel marvelled at Ella's performance. He had stopped counting her orgasms aloud, but they were all down on paper. He cast an eye over the computer printout. The graph of his captive's sexual energy showed an inexorable downward trend. Little peaks superimposed on this trend marked her orgasms, and he counted. There had been thirty-four, in a period of five hours! It was phenomenal! And now all that energy was his to exploit.

He had already come three times himself, he was so enthralled with the success of his equipment. A fourth, and he would go to bed. He signalled to his squaw, who was dressed now in a designer Cheyenne two-piece bathing costume, and she bent over tirelessly to take his cock in her mouth again.

Carnel studied the graph, and his cock surged to life on pure greed. His top-security sex-tech lab had come up trumps. Thirty-four orgasms in five hours, and after every one, an irreversible plunge. He read the data on his orgone capacitor. This remarkable machine had taken from its subject fifteen mega-Reichs of orgone energy and put fourteen-and-a-half into storage. It ran on almost nothing!

The squaw pumped with her hand as she sucked.

Carnel flicked a switch which sent the machine into a new, and final mode. Already the energy of the subject woman had fallen below the level at which she could ever regain her function as a sexual being. Just like a rechargeable battery, Carnel thought simplistically. Drain them too low and they're junk.

He trusted his boffins implicitly. They had proved themselves magnificently. He could dump the woman somewhere out of the way and she would remain sexless to her dying day. But he was a penny-pincher. And the squaw was waiting for him. So he set the machine to take every last nano-Reich from Ella Deedes.

Georgey Porgey advanced brazenly. There were no moving pictures and no music. Ella closed her eyes and waited.

The silence and the darkness were profound. Just the silent, invisible bustle of the machine. Ella could sense its excitement.

Georgey squirted liquid over her crotch and bottom, and two of his pads spread it around. It felt to Ella as though she was being lathered. Then he paused, as if taking a deep breath. And then he advanced on her.

She felt two enormous plastic clamps surround her vulva and bottom, meeting between her legs, and moulding precisely to the contours of her flesh. The vice holding her hips and waist, the sensors and activators fastened to her breasts and other erogenous zones, all became as one. All were perfectly lubricated. All made perfect contact with her sexual pores. Georgey had her in total embrace. Slowly, with great gentleness and the appropriate stimulator in each place, he wooed her seven orifices. He penetrated the lower two. And he took from her. He won her willing consent, even her encouragement. But the transmission of energy was in one direction only.

Blas Carnel watched as the continuous printout of Ella's sexual energy dived to absolute zero and stayed there. The computer bleeped three times, as if asking to be shut off.

After thirty-four *petits morts* in five hours, Ella had lived through *le grand mort* and was left as a sexless shadow of her former self.

Carnel shot his sperm into his squaw's mouth with consummate satisfaction.

'Time to hit the hay, honey,' he said. 'We'll leave her on this programme once an hour until morning, just to make sure. Then we'll decide what to do with the empty shell.'

8

TAKING THE ROUGH WITH THE SMOOTH

It's time to start playing, Ella told herself.

She wanted to sleep. She wanted to be alone. But she was still tied, hand and foot. And she knew they would be back. She was still their plaything.

I've got to go out and do the playing, she told herself again. But it was pitch black and silent. How could she play? What was there left to play?

Forget the voice behind the glass. He must have had enough by now. He was probably tucked in bed with his teddy. And there was no one else. She'd been put in a 'safe' room. She was cut off from everybody.

Everybody except . . . Georgey Porgey!

Ella cast her mind back over the films she had seen. There had been no sex with robots; not the slightest suggestion of cybernetic eroticism. Here was a game *she* could play.

But where was he? Ella closed her eyes again and pictured the little fellow as she had last seen him. She embraced his body in her mind, her soft naked flesh pressing with a thrill against his hard steel skin. She imagined her curvaceous limbs wrapping themselves like loving tentacles around his hard straight lines and rigid corners, her breathing pores like sensory suckers. The vigorous curly hairs of her fuzz-bush scratched against his perfect smoothness as she dragged her lower lips up his flank and left in their wake a trail of scented juices, then slid down to latch on his power point . . . as the lips of her mouth pressed their full-blooded flesh against his mechanical arm, the tip of her

109

tongue tracing its long inflexible length to its operative probe, and then her mouth taking it inside, to play with it.

She opened her eyes. At first she thought it was her imagination still at play. But soon she was convinced of the reality. Georgey Porgey had got the hots! He was emitting a faint but steady glow! And he was moving towards her . . .

She couldn't tell if he was responding to her fantasy, or if this was simply the next stage of his programme. So she spoke to him. She rolled and pursed her lips, wet them with the tip of her tongue, and invested the simple words, 'Come here' . . . 'Come to me' 'Come!' with all the sexual appeal she could muster.

The probe which was level with her crotch seemed to rise up fractionally. She recognised it as the same as last time; the one with the aperture at the end; the one which had lathered her. She seduced it with her mouth and watched it raise itself reluctantly, as if restrained by . . . duty? Probity? Guilt? Ella threw herself into her role and on it came, and higher it rose.

At last, straining forward as far as she could, Ella reached the tip of the probe with her tongue. She was sure the glow from the body proper pulsed with a higher intensity. She sucked him towards her, wrapped her lips around the cold metal, and made love with her mouth.

Within seconds she felt a warm liquid shooting from the hole at the tip of the probe. It was the lubricant, a viscous fluid with a slightly musky odour and bitter taste. She closed her mouth to it and the lotion meant for her crotch slithered down Georgey's own arm, its magic working on him instead. Ella could feel the effect. The probe felt hotter as she fellated it. The diffuse glow seemed to concentrate in this one adjunct, this organ, this member, until she had to close her mouth again, or else get burned!

She screamed sex at it. Touch, she said. The power of touch could kindle a light Georgey had never known before. If only he could feel the magic of her touch, the heat of her hand. And she willed the probe onwards, up the length of her arm, towards her fettered hand.

It worked.

In the control room the computer monitoring the orgone capacitor bleeped once, as if in surprise. But there was no one there to hear it. The one-half mega-Reich of orgone energy which fuelled the machine had been used to open the valve and now energy was being drained back out of Carnel's storage bank.

Georgey Porgey's dick was getting too hot to handle! Ella's shackled fingers danced their best around its surface and drew it close against the fabric of the bond which held her wrist. She could smell the material getting singed. She pulled away. She was getting scorched by her own sexual energy! She jerked her hand away again, and the weakened tie broke. Her hand was free!

Immediately she stroked the lower reaches of the probe, smoothing down the energy concentrated in the head and diffusing it to lower the heat. She smiled with confidence. This was her game now and she was going to enjoy it. But she had to keep the initiative and move fast.

She carefully pulled back the tape which held a sensor on her right nipple. Keeping the wires intact, she quickly dabbed the end of the device between her labia, smearing it with what remained of her vaginal juices. Then she stuck it on Georgey's breast, and taped it down.

In the deserted control room a red light flashed unobserved on the monitor.

With her one free hand Ella detached all the sensors from her own body, endowed them with a taste of her sex, and re-attached them on the robot. Instinct guided her to his erogenous zones. And surges in the intensity of his body-glow assured her that her instincts in such matters were still intact.

Then she swiftly unfastened her other bonds. She rubbed her stiff and sore points, stretched her unused muscles and shook herself down. Then she found her Indian-cowgirl outfit in the corner and put it on. She tried the door. It was unlocked.

But the machine was moving towards her with a possessive, demanding mien. She wrapped her bare arms around the solid metal trunk and hugged tight, pushing her bosom flat against it. Then she lifted one leg and wrapped it around the lower part, the soft leather fringes of the squaw leggings swishing against shiny steel. She hitched up her skirt at the front so her pubic hair could scratch the stainless skin, and she pressed again in a tight embrace to kiss him with her lower lips. On the other side of the one-way glass the bleeping became so insistent that Ella could hear it.

'I'd like to win your heart and soul, too,' she whispered to the object of her bodily caress. 'But I must dash.'

She reached for the two dildolike probes and with one in each hand she quickly explored the unfamiliar surface of the lower rear body of the machine. She found two sockets, stretched the probes to the limit of their flexible armatures, and lovingly inserted them.

There was a radical change in the auralike glow. Was it steam, hissing from hairline joints? Or the silicon chip equivalent of hair standing on end? The continuous bleeping sound in the control room rose to the level of an alarm.

Ella gave her Georgey Porgey an affectionate peck on the forehead and fled.

With the stealth of an Apache prisoner fleeing a cavalry fort, Ella had traversed the deserted hallway outside the technosex-lab, located the back door of the manor and crossed the open yard. But once in the woods she had lost her cool and run in a wild panic. Within minutes she had tripped over a root and fallen headlong into a patch of brambles, scratching her face and hands. Then she thought she heard dogs coming after her and in trying to climb up into a young pine she tore her leggings and bruised her shin. And when she finally made it to the perimeter wall she was in such a blind rush to get over, she caught the back of her skirt on the barbed wire and ripped a six-inch slit in it.

On the roadside Ella felt no safer. It was still early morning and there was very little traffic. At the sound of the first vehicle, frightened that the alarm had been raised and they were after her, she dived into the ditch. She stumbled out with nettle stings up both arms and burrs in her hair, too late to flag down the milk van. The next time she took her chance and stuck out her thumb.

It was a farm truck heading for market and Ella spent the duration of the ride insisting that she had not been raped. Or at least, that she didn't want him to drive her straight to the nearest hospital.

The second trucker, who took her fifty miles from Pod Magna to the motorway, gave her the address of a battered wives refuge and pressed a fiver into her hand for a taxi.

Then she picked up a ride going all the way to London.

'How!' said the driver, as Ella climbed up into his cab. 'You squaw: me big chief!'

'Yeah,' she answered. 'But I'm a renegade fresh off the reservation and if you so much as touch me, Big Boy, I'll scalp your pubes and hang your balls from my bracelet.'

Ella woke a restful three hours later when the driver set her down at the entrance to New Covent Garden. She took a taxi to the City. And there she was pounced on by a bored press corps convinced she was about to pull a hot stunt at the expense of a multinational mining company which was exploiting the Lakota Nation. They got pictures of every scratch and bruise, and the six-inch slit in the miniskirt, against a backdrop of macho hustle on the jobber's floor. But she said she couldn't give them a story until she'd found Goode and at last one of them arranged for her to meet a man who might be able to help.

It was only a short walk to his office, and a hardcore of pressmen followed her. But the man in question met Ella in the lobby and insisted she leave her entourage there. He showed her to the lift, stepped in behind her, and within a second of the door closing he had his cock out of his fly and was rubbing it up against her leather skirt.

'Speed the plough!' Ella said with amusement. But she pushed him back by the shoulders. 'Where's Goode?'

'He was here last night, with a bunch of girls.' The man lunged forward with his crotch. Ella could see that he was coming, and that he was desperate to touch the leather.

'Where'd they go?'

He gabbled his answer: 'The Magna Carta, I think. In Soho. Or maybe Zedekiah's.'

She let go his shoulders and he rubbed against her once

before splattering his sperm on the front of her skirt. The lift sighed to a halt as the man tucked his dick away.

But Ella held her hand firmly over the doors-closed button and then pressed Ground. 'I'm supposed to wear my stains like wounds, and my wounds like medals, am I?'

But Quickie Dickie couldn't handle two rides in the lift on a row. An unprecedented five seconds of his working life were spent doing nothing. He simply gaped at her, speechlessly. As the lift reached ground level Ella rubbed her crotch against his flank, smearing his sperm on to his dark blue pinstripe suit.

'True blue never stains,' she laughed. She gave him a peck on the cheek as the doors opened, and a couple of cameras flashed from the lobby. Then she swept on her way leaving him to answer the questions.

The trail was still hot in Soho. Goode and his bevy of beauties had made an impression in every bar and club they visited. There was a hiccup when Ella was given a lead to a man called Baby James. She couldn't get past his secretary, a dominating and overprotective motherly type who insisted that he didn't need another change yet and she was quite capable of providing it herself when he did. But Ella sidestepped James when she clued on to Toni: a stunner who didn't blabber, a flash girl who let it come to her, and a work number back in the City. Ella knew she was getting close.

Tony took a shine to Ella and insisted she join him for lunch. He looked thirties-style American gangster with wide lapels, turn-ups and sleeked down hair, and Ella got the size of him at once. She ordered buffalo steak with pemmican, and they both laughed.

When they finished eating, Tony topped up Ella's taxi money. One of the fivers had Goode's address on it.

'He gave it me last thing,' he said wistfully.

Ella asked if he had copied it down, or memorised it.

Tony shook his head and smiled. 'It's not necessarily wise to try and relive past triumphs.'

Ella insisted he write his own number on the note. 'We'll join forces and go on the warpath together sometime.'

He gave her a sisterly smile. 'Send me a smoke signal and I'll come.'

A cleaning lady let Ella in at Goode's place and nodded towards the bedroom door without batting an eye.

It was dark and hot in the room and Ella stood quietly just inside the door until her senses adapted. There appeared to be a heap of sexual spaghetti on the king-sized double bed. Then she started to differentiate lumps in the tangled sprawl of naked limbs, the breasts and buttocks of an Italianate sauce. There was just one cock and it looked as battered, bruised and exhausted as Ella herself.

She sat in an armchair at the foot of the bed and waited. Goode was lying spread-eagled on his back in the centre of the bed. A tall, thin woman with long black hair lay facing him on one side, curled around his head so that her breasts nestled against his face, and her thighs wrapped around his forearm. A flashy blonde with gold bangles round her ankles and wrists lay on the other side, her head on Goode's chest in a pose suggesting possession, not surrender. The third lay crosswise across the bottom of the bed, over one of the hairy male limbs and under the other, her big boobs squashed up against his balls. The other feminine legs lay across or against her in mutual comfort, her dainty flesh yielding unthinkingly, like a pretty bolster.

'Tell her to go away,' Fiona said without opening her eyes.

Without moving anything but her eyelids, Melissa looked at Ella.

'Tell her to do this room tomorrow.'

'It's not her,' Melissa said.

Fiona opened one eye and stared at Melissa. Then she whispered threateningly: 'Tell her he's ours! We're not giving him up, ever.'

Melissa repeated the message and added unnecessarily 'There's no room.'

And then Lallie made a snorelike noise and twitched. Melissa poked at the girl's bum with her foot and Fiona said, 'She's dreaming . . . imagining what it's like to have him come inside her, poor thing.'

Lallie woke like Vesuvius.

There followed a five-minute romp during which Goode argued, implored, made promises, threatened, pinched bottoms, wrestled, spanked, and finally succeeded in shooing his companions of the night out of his room. Ella watched with uncharacteristic indifference. Was it the importance of her mission, weighing on her? Or was she simply exhausted, drained? And if so, in what way? She didn't want to put herself to the test.

'You just met Greedy, Catty and Bitchy,' Goode said, with a charming smile.

Ella simply shrugged her shoulders. Goode strolled to the window and raised the blind to let a little light into the room. Ella winced.

'Good heavens!' He dropped the blind at once. 'What on earth has happened to you?'

And at last she started talking.

He locked the door, poured her a double brandy from the bedside cabinet and started filling the tub in the *en suite* bathroom. He listened to her story as he ministered to her immediate needs and believed every word of it. He believed, but couldn't comprehend. There was a world of difference between what had clearly happened to Ella and her hypotheses about what was going on.

He carefully lifted Ella's arms one at a time and eased the tattered Indian shift up over her head. He knelt at her feet and tugged off the boots. Then he loosened the beadwork garters and tried to slide her leggings down but she flinched in pain. So he fetched a pair of sharp scissors from the bedroom and cut the material from her legs. He unfastened the belt round her skirt and then pulled her to her feet. The skirt fell to her ankles and Ella stepped out of it.

Goode quickly rubbed a dab of comfrey ointment on each of her cuts and bruises. Then he led her to the bath and helped her climb in. He poured a capful of orange and almond oil into the deep, hot water and climbed in behind her, cradling her back with one leg each side of her. He gently massaged her shoulders while he tried desperately to remember what Toni had told him.

After a long luxurious soak, Goode wet Ella's hair and

massaged her scalp with his fingertips. She felt looser and more relaxed in his hands. He reached behind him for a bottle of massage lotion and dropped it in the bathwater to warm the contents.

'The man behind this business is called Blas Carnel,' Goode said aloud as it suddenly came back to him. He thought Ella nodded. 'He's an extremely wealthy American. In communications.'

But Ella was past communicating now, and Goode decided to take her in hand again. He rinsed off her body, dried himself quickly, and then hooked a huge fluffy bath towel out of the warming cupboard. He pulled her up out of the water and enveloped her in the warm soft fabric, dabbing her dry without rubbing. He steered her back to the bedroom, whipped a quilt out of the blanket chest to spread on the floor, and laid her face down on it, still wrapped in the towel.

He knelt at her feet again, and reached one hand up under the extravagant towelling to find a foot. He kept contact with this hand, stroking and squeezing the warm flesh of Ella's foot, while with his other hand he expertly unscrewed the lid of the massage lotion and opened the aromatherapy kit his sister had left behind on her last visit.

Goode scanned the chart on the inside of the lid. 'To reduce anxiety . . . basil.' He found the appropriate tiny bottle and using the dropper fastened to the lid, added a tiny measure to the lotion. 'To combat fatigue . . . rosemary.' In it went. He felt like a sorcerer. Three drops of bergamot, 'which is especially uplifting', and ten drops of ylang-ylang. His eye had caught the footnote: 'long used as an aphrodisiac'.

He was ready to start. He poured a pool of lotion on to the palm of his hand and rubbed it soothingly up and down the length of his penis, around his balls, and along both creases of his pelvis.

Now he was ready to give. He slid the towel up over Ella's legs to reveal both feet and calves. With more lotion on his hands he stroked and smoothed her legs down to her feet. Then he lifted one foot at a time on to his lap, pressed both his thumbs into the flesh of its heel and played them back and forth, rolling them, circling slightly, covering the entire surface again and again. Her breathing became slower and deeper until he worried briefly that it had ceased altogether, her only audible sign of life returning more as a pulsing groan of contentment.

He ran his thumbs forcefully along her instep to the ball of her foot and began a new cycle of massage, pressing up with his fingertips on one side as he worked his thumbs into the sole on the other. He felt her softness and her profound trust in him. He tugged gently on each toe, sliding an oily finger in and out between them. Then he tugged on the whole foot, cradling the arch in his left hand and cupping his right around the heel. He pulled slowly and firmly, then relaxed. Pulled slowly, then relaxed. Seven times.

He massaged the second foot as thoroughly and tenderly as the first. He felt he was drawing her energy down to earth, so that she could put her scattered thoughts and wild hypotheses on a solid footing. But as he did so he felt a growing sexual charge in his hands. He was consolidating her sexual energy, too; clearing away confusion, concentrating, restoring . . . And he believed he had never before beheld such beautiful forms, such sensual shapes. He made love to her feet with his hands. They became the most gorgeous symbols of sexual promise, with their inviting curves and tendons flexed, their delicate ankles, spreading toes and the sweep of arched instep which was the gush and thrust of orgasm set in flesh and bone, the sculptural essence of Eros.

He sprinkled talc on the oiled feet, rubbed them dry, and then kissed them, blindly. He spread his lips round each ankle bone in turn and sucked; ran his tongue down the soft spaces between tendons; took the big toe deep in his mouth and made love to it with his lips and his tongue. She was gorgeous! She was adorable! And she was indescribably sexy!

Goode couldn't imagine why he had not made love to her before, why he had not fallen for her at once. And he was forced to confront again the strange asexuality of Pod Parva and Ella's bizarre notions about what was going on.

He knelt alongside her and pulled the towel up to her

waist. He began a meticulous ascent by massage, starting with little stretching circles around the ankle bones, then over the bare wold of her calves, through the sloping vales behind the knees, up the escarpment of her thighs. He paused to sweep the energy back down to her feet, with long smooth strokes from thigh to toe, keeping her grounded. And then he started rolling the flesh of her right thigh between his hands, one starting on the inside and the other outside, passing with a delectable squeeze and then returning higher up. The hand which dipped away on the inside brushed at last against pubic hair and then moved on to her buttocks.

Ella felt herself stretched. But what a different kind of stretch this time! Earthed in herself, feet grounded . . . and her spirit free, zooming heavenwards.

'It's something to do with telecommunications,' Goode said, thinking aloud. 'And advertising. Something new and very big.'

He had started a squashing movement, squeezing the flesh of her bottom cheeks between his thumbs and fingertips and stretching it sideways. Then he switched to a percussive movement, raining down a barrage of light blows with the sides of his hands. Her bottom was soon aglow with pleasure, her crotch engorged and hot with anticipation. His hands moved up her back, still sweeping down at frequent intervals, loosening and dissolving her tension and anxiety, shifting her jitters. He was shifting her jitters to her crotch, restoring her balance.

Goode pushed her legs apart and knelt between them, facing her bottom. He poured a thin stream of oil on to the crease between her cheeks and she felt it trickle down the crack and soak into her crotch. She felt his fingers following the oil. Then he pushed her thighs further apart with his knees and she felt warm, oily flesh penetrating her vagina.

He had slid two fingers inside her, palm down towards the floor, and he was exploring the front wall of her vagina for her G-spot. He was pressing hard and her pubic bone ground against the hard surface beneath the thin quilt. He found the small hard lump. As he pressed harder, it started to swell. Ella felt a burning sensation. He was pressing near the neck of her bladder and it felt like she needed to pee. Then he pressed harder than ever. The spot was as big as a ten pence piece. The pissing sensation passed and in its place Ella experienced sheer pleasure – intense, extreme, almost unendurable pleasure! The two fingers hardly moved, just pinned her to the floor, and she felt the first twinge in her womb. Gee, but it was deep. Her orgasm galloped towards her. Gee, but she was full! Full of sex! Bursting with it! Enough to ejaculate!

She spat out a dab of milky fluid. Goode whipped out his fingers and slammed in his cock. As it slithered up and down her vagina his pubic bone pounded against her bottom, his hair rustling her hot oily cheeks. He fucked hard and fast and in seconds his milky fluid shot out to swim with hers.

Goode collapsed on top of Ella, curling his groin around her luscious, fulsome bottom and planting a single appreciative kiss between her shoulder blades. Then he rolled on his side, pulling her with him, and came out of her in a smooth, graceful movement, easing her over even further so that she lay on her back.

She was like painting in oils after sketching with coloured pencils. Goode sat at her feet again, took one of them into his lap, and repeated the massage. She was like jamming on tenor sax after playing nursery rhymes on a descant recorder. He would have to send her back to Pod Parva: he had promised the old man. And now he wanted to go with her. That meant dealing with whatever was going on, whether it was on the ground or in her head.

Ella was happy to let him play. She soaked up his artistry and revelled in his touch. There would be time to have him properly later.

Goode's hands functioned instinctively as he racked his brain again in search of the information Toni had given him.

'It's all to do with a new way of giving adverts sex appeal,' he said. He moved up her shins and over her knees. 'Something about sending out TV ads with a kind of sex appeal.' As he leaned forward to massage her thighs, Ella felt a hard, hot rod of flesh touch her briefly. He was far from finished, she realised with delight and some surprise, so that the import of his words did not strike her at first.

'But it's still hush-hush. If it works it will be worth billions.' His hands reached her crotch. 'That's all I learned.'

He gave her a superb genital massage. After the G-spot orgasm, a clitoral orgasm, Ella presumed. And then a third? But he slid his penis into her vagina and slowly rocked it back and forth, while his fingers still rubbed her clitoris. Two and three were going to come together.

But not so swiftly! While his cock drove in and out of her cunt and one hand played with her clitoris, the other poured oil on her breasts and fondled them. He must be balanced on his knees, she thought, one leg astride hers. But she abandoned herself to the sensation without puzzling it out. The hand on her breasts was sliding down her flank, and on down her thigh. Then back to her breasts. He was earthing her again! Earth and heaven, both at once! And as she rushed towards her many faceted climax, she made an intuitive leap. Heaven and earth! Blas Carnel was beaming down sexual energy from the heavens, along with satellite TV, and he was getting it from earth . . . from the sexual sump in Pod Parva! It was brilliant. It was devious. It was mean, greedy, cruel. Of course it would be worth billions!

They came together, with perfect timing.

She would have to go straight back to the village, she realised. Only she was immune. But she hoped now that she could work with Goode, too. She would take this darling oversexed bimbo who doubled as nature diarist and sketcher of birds with her. And as soon as she got there she would put him to the test.

9

DING DONG BELL

The customised Cadillac swept towards London. For three hours or more it became the nerve centre of SMIPT: strategic HQ and battlefield command post. It was driven by Head of Security, suitably subdued, and on the seat beside him rode Personnel, similarly long in the face. In the screened and secretive rear, the personal assistant in immaculate squaw outfit sat beside an unusually aroused and invigorated Blas Carnel. He was wearing the world's biggest ten-gallon hat and he put down the phone like a man jumping off the gate of the big corral at the start of a rodeo.

'Yipee! Let's ride!'

'You've found her?'

'She's in London for sure. We've got to go see a no-good limey jobber in a goddamned elevator. Pass me a beer.'

Carnel's new sex robot had taken a battering and his monitoring equipment was on the blink. But his technomen said it could all be put right in twenty-four hours. God knows how the freak-girl had done it, but he was sure she was a loner, a maverick, a renegade . . . his instincts told him so, and it was his instinct that had made him what he was. It just proved what he had always known, that when it came right down to it you had to have a real man in the saddle. Someone with a cool head. A troubleshooter.

'Now we'll play cowboys 'n' Injuns!' he said with glee.

The PA opened up the TV screen and unzipped Carnel's fly. She reached two fingers in and searched out the head of his cock which was curled up fast asleep.

'When the goddamned computer crashes,' he said, 'you've got to know you've got a real tool you can fall back on.' He knocked back his beer. He was in command, like in the good old days, and he was sure as hell going to hunt down that girl and scalp her!

His squaw had found some ads on satellite TV. His sleeping cock woke up and stretched. A picture of baked beans was raising a beam! It was giving him a blue veiner . . . He was still in business!

The PA's hand closed on his long thick cock and started sliding the surface skin up and down over the engorged, throbbing shaft. Business was what it was all about, Carnel reminded himself, but commerce was a complicated business these days. He could pin the nuisance girl himself, but it might be prudent to enlist a little backup security. It was high time SMIPT recruited a few friends in the legislature, in the judiciary, and among the agents of law enforcement. Goddamn, it was getting exciting!

'What the hell, let's shoot on the next one, honey.' He reached for the phone again and the hand around his cock moved up and down more vigorously while the mouth came down to take him.

As the Cadillac and its preoccupied passengers approached the home counties, an open-top MG passed them going in the opposite direction. Behind the wheel, an inordinately cheerful youth who looked like he'd just won the national lottery; and beside him another with the air of a childhood sweetheart reluctant to say goodbye to the simple joys and certainties of their small-time life together.

Ella had made a remarkable recovery since Goode's ministrations of the early afternoon. He had taken her down Oxford Street and she had bought a gorgeous frock which fitted her like a dream. It had a long, full skirt, tight bodice, and short puffy sleeves and she was wearing it barefoot and without underwear. She felt like a Cossack peasant in high summer. The airstream blew her hair forward and it lashed a face rosy and warm in the setting sun. She wanted to keep Goode close to earth.

They reached Pod Magna at dusk and drove on from there down a tiny lane unfamiliar to Ella. Goode parked in a derelict barn with all the confidence of a man with a plan.

He took Ella by the hand and led her across a meadow, alongside a copse of birch and willow, then up a tree and through a trapdoor into his favourite hide.

'We're safe as houses,' he boasted.

She put it to him as gently as she could that they didn't come here to be safe. But he was busy showing her the features, as though they were newlyweds in their first home. 'And we're only a mile and a half from the village,' he said, as though comforting her with the proximity of all amenities.

Ella leaned on the parapet and looked out. The hide was made of rough logs which felt good under her naked feet. It was solid on all sides up to four feet then open all round up to a token roof at standing height. Night was gathering fast and there was little to see. But Ella stood entranced. There was certainly plenty to hear, and she knew with a sympathy that was not merely human but cosmic in its scope that these were the noises of sex. She imagined a host of insects, fucking away. She pictured fat female frogs grabbed by males, front and back at the same time; and roly-poly little mammals at it in the hedgerows and ditches. She listened to all that chirruping and croaking and she felt herself open so that she was breathing in every pore of her body. She was breathing through her armpits, through the soles of her feet . . . breathing in the healthy rank odour of noisy outdoor night-time sex.

Still leaning on the parapet and without turning round, Ella slowly hitched up her skirt at the back; up over her round buttocks. She stretched high on her toes, leaning forward, rubbing her clitoris through her dress on the edge of the shelf and thrusting her bare bottom out behind her. She was open and breathing and alive, sharing in the feast of blind display which was all around her.

She felt two cold hands on her hips, and the touch of rough fabric against her bottom. 'Cock, cock . . .' she mouthed, and the hands fell away. She didn't turn. She just kept rubbing herself. She closed her eyes and joined the blind, croaking chorus: 'Cock . . . cock . . . cock!' And then the touch came back, hot, pressing hard against the line between her cheeks. She felt one cold hand against the top of her left thigh, the other feeling between her legs. It made her gasp, but all she could say was 'Cock!' and then the cold tentative touch gave way to a hot certainty. She could smell it, sharp and fishlike. 'Cock, cock,' she moaned with sweet insistence. And with all the swiftness she demanded, the stiff penis advanced between the plump folds of her buttocks and pushed its way to her vaginal lips. It drove straight on through her soft, tender opening, up her mucous-slimy, smooth interior. 'Cock!' she kept grunting in imperative time with the quick deep thrusts inside her. 'Cock! Cock! Cock! . . .' Until her face twisted with the urgency of timing and she gripped this thick hot thing inside her, contorting with effort as she came came came . . . hugging the thing inside her and shouting 'Cock!' with her last desperate breath because she wanted its sour cream . . . and out it came in a great leap, squirting inside her . . . and then oozing out, and dribbling down her leg.

The two dark figures stayed frozen in animal union as if powerless to move until triggered by some ritual or hormonal shift beyond their control. Then the moon came up, above the tops of the trees.

Ella pulled herself off him and let her skirt fall down around her.

'This place is lovely, George,' she said. 'Really lovely. But I'm afraid it just won't do.'

She picked up the bag he had brought with emergency supplies, and strung his binoculars with her camera round her neck. Then she took him forcibly by the hand and led him back down through the trapdoor to the ground. She asked him the direction to Pod Parva and set off across country.

When the first houses came into view Ella stopped to listen. She climbed a fence on to a lane and stopped again. It was late and there was no sound of people or vehicles. But she moved ahead more furtively. George had followed her mindlessly and as they came to The Row he broke away and headed towards his cottage. Ella grabbed his shirt-tail and pulled him back, with a finger across her lips commanding silence. She took his hand and made her way swiftly, in the night-shadow of the dark buildings, to the church. She paused briefly in the seclusion of the lychgate to reconnoitre the last stretch of open ground, and then made a dash through the graveyard to the church door.

By the filtered moonlight inside the church Ella eventually found a small door which led to the tower. She was startled in the anteroom by a row of choristers . . . a line of their white-and-black gowns, hanging from a rack, swayed towards her in the draught caused by the opened door. 'We'll borrow a few to keep us warm,' she told Goode. 'Don't get them dirty.' And then they climbed the tiny spiral staircase.

Passing three small doors on their way up, they emerged eventually on the roof of the tower, and made their bed. Ella peeped out from the crenellated turret to the sleeping village below and expressed her satisfaction. Goode gazed up at the stars and contemplated his eventful day. He didn't know yet whether the two worlds he inhabited had been happily joined together or split asunder and wrecked for ever.

They fell asleep in each other's arms.

Blas Carnel sent one of his henchmen up to the club on the top floor, with a note for the limey jobber. The other one stayed with him and his PA in the lobby. Two minutes later, the lift came down and the personal assistant got in with a puzzled Quickie Dickie. The heavy at the top and the heavy at the bottom made sure there were no interruptions and Carnel sat back and watched the indicator lights going up, and then down.

Eight times the lift went up and down, and then Carnel let it stop at the bottom and the doors opened.

The girl stepped out smiling, smoothing down the front of her leather tunic with her hand. In the corner, the gent from the city looked devastated. He lay slumped on the floor, his trousers round his ankles, cordless phone jammed between his legs, his little willy seeping out a last drop of clear, thin liquid as if begging tearfully for mercy.

'Nice ride, buddy?' Carnel counted three different pools of sperm on the lift floor. 'Riding the elevator, eh? Up and down and up and down and up and down. That's a boy!'

The girl told him the name of a club in Soho and Carnel nodded his approval. It was going to be a long night, perhaps, but one way or another he was going to enjoy it.

Ella and Goode woke simultaneously with a clang. It was a very deep, very loud clang and it threw them hard together. Then came more clangs, louder still, metallic, even through the choristers' robes which Goode pulled around their heads to muffle the sound. It became a din, a cacophony of unconnected noise, macho-loud but nattery.

'They're ringing the bells,' Goode said unnecessarily.

Then silence returned, like a French kiss.

'They've lifted them.'

Ella jumped to her feet and ran down the spiral staircase until she came to one of the little side doors. It opened on a chamber with louvred windows containing eight bells of different sizes, all enormous. They were now pointing upwards, the yokes to which they were fastened caught against a wooden bar. Goode poked his head in behind her.

'Is that it?' she asked.

'Hardly, my dear. It's not Sunday, which means they're doing this for fun. On eight bells you can ring forty thousand, three hundred and twenty changes without repeating a single one.'

A thick rope running close by the largest bell started to move, the huge wooden wheel around which it passed began to rotate, and the bell itself leaned, tottered and tumbled. Even before the clapper struck, Ella was aware of the other ropes moving, wheels turning. It was like a great beast limbering up and lurching into movement.

'It's all very mechanical, very mathematical,' Goode said hurriedly, while he could still be heard. 'I read up about it for one of your traditional English customs.'

Ella made a viewfinder with her fingers, trying to get a feel for it.

'Handel called it our national instrument.'

Then with every muscle and limb on its own efficient course, all coordinated with perfect timing, the beast began to dance. And as it danced, it sang. Here was a giant mechanical contraption, thrust up in the air as though trying to reach heaven, dancing on the end of ropes like a puppet upside down, defying gravity. And it was making the music of the spheres! Ella thrilled to it with all her senses. Even her crotch vibrated in sympathy.

Goode pulled her out of the chamber and led her down another stage to the room immediately below. It housed the clock, with faces on four walls, its workings running well clear of the eight bell-ropes which stretched from holes in the floor to holes in the ceiling. Ella risked a rope burn on her nose and peered down through one of the holes. There were six men and two women below, pulling rhythmically on their ropes. They appeared to be in a trance, drugged by their sound and their sums. Dead pictures, Ella thought. But she knew how to bring them to life.

She told Goode. 'I'll show you the power of SMIPT's snivelling little scheme, and how it can be broken.' She cast around for a fantasy. Hanging from the wall behind the ringers she saw a set of eight hand bells of different sizes.

'You see the little bells?' she said. 'I'll show you how different a tune they can play on our sweet little village green.'

They went back to the roof and ate an uninspiring breakfast out of Goode's bags. Ella pointed to the dip in the green where the pond used to be. 'I'll make for there as quickly as possible, just in case someone from SMIPT is on the lookout. But you can watch; that's one of the reasons I chose this place.' She patted the binoculars and smiled. 'Watch and enjoy yourself.'

Ella lay back with her face towards the climbing sun and closed her eyes. She listened to the ringing bells and sought inspiration.

'The fantasy is important, I'm sure,' she mused aloud for Goode's benefit. 'But you've got to keep it loose, and full of possibilities, so you can be accommodating.'

She gently rubbed her clitoris through the material of her dress while picturing her breasts as little hand bells, her erect nipples their handles. A male hand was ringing her bells . . . then a tongue . . . then the tongue became the clanger, and then was replaced by a stiff cock. She played with the idea of cock as clanger . . . a man's dong . . . ding dong bell . . . and now *she* was playing *them*. She had her men with bells on their cocks and to her stimulus, at her command, they played their tune and rang their changes. That was another phrase to conjure with. From her breasts as bells she jumped with exciting surreal imagery to buttocks as bells . . . round and deep-toned . . . with cocks as the clangers to play them . . . and never a dull moment, always ringing the changes . . . making the mechanical into the sublime.

She was wet between the legs with anticipation.

The moment the ringing stopped she told Goode to watch from the clock room first, and she dashed down the stairs with her camera at the ready. She reached the door to the ringing chamber just as it opened, and acted as though she had come up from the church.

'Such a lovely sound,' she said. 'We don't have anything like it in the States. Could I take a picture?'

But most of them were in a rush. They had jobs to go to. They filed past brusquely and by the time she had the door closed with her back against it, only the village schoolmaster and his nephew, who was lodging with him for the summer, remained. One was a very well preserved forty-five, the other in his early twenties. Both were unduly sombre and ridiculously shy, but underneath their sexless exterior Ella liked what she saw.

She bullied them into posing with their hands above their heads on the bell ropes. She put their limbs in place herself, and rubbed her breasts and crotch against them in doing so. But not a rise did she get out of them. She brushed her hand down over their cocks to check.

She said it was so cosy in the windowless room; warm and snug and private. She fanned out her skirt to show her thighs, and then pulled her bodice away from her breasts right in front of them, to show how warm she was. She could sense Goode's eye on her, and feel him burning up. But these two were frozen silly. She suggested they could have some private fun and games if they liked, just the three of them. And she got the distinct impression that they didn't know what she was talking about.

'OK, guys,' she said, as though happy to let them go. 'Just one last shot of you holding those little hand bells with the big bells off in the background.'

'How do we do that?' the nephew asked.

Ella winked at him. 'By standing out on the village green, with the church tower behind you.'

They carried two bells each and Ella took a man on each arm so she could set the pace. As soon as she was on the green she said she thought they had been very rude to her in the church and before she shot the picture she insisted they show her how to play the bells, and there was a little dip in the ground just ahead where they could sit for a while and not disturb anyone.

The teacher apologised profusely and assured her that he had meant no offence. The nephew asked if he could carry her bells for her.

When they reached the dell of the old pond, Ella sat facing the tower and the two men facing her, but with a space between them. All she could see of the village was the top of the church tower, but see it she plainly could. She was going to enjoy playing to the gallery as well as the front stalls.

The teacher had arranged the six bells in order of size on the grass in front of him and was giving an enthusiastic lecture about how to dodge 1-2 up if a bob is called with the treble in the middle of the front work. The nephew was simply ogling Ella's bosom.

'Yes,' Ella said, with a lovely disarming smile as she reached for the two largest bells. 'But how would you play them here?' She pressed the domes of the bells down around her breasts, fitting them snugly over the bodice of her dress and then wriggling her bosom out to fill them.

The nephew reached a hand up to the bell nearest him and held it in place by the small wooden handle. Then he gently pressed, twisted back and forth, and gyrated his instrument. Ella smiled and looked questioningly at the teacher. His hand too, took to this new way of playing the bells. Ella tilted her head back, smiling, and pushed her breasts out to meet their playful moves. She groaned with pleasure and excitement. There was no rush now. Time stood still for this kind of play.

All the same, after a few minutes she spoke again, without ceasing her reciprocal movement, and with her eyes closed.

'Yes . . . Yes . . . Play my bells! Ring my tits! Ring my sex! Yes . . . Yes . . . But it's only fair that I should ring your bells too.'

She came back to the vertical and slid their hands away from the bells, holding them in place herself and continuing their sensual movement. 'It's much more comfortable barefoot, like me. So why don't you take off your socks and shoes?' She waited patiently. 'And then kneel in front of me.' She cupped the bells on them, one on the teacher and one on the nephew, and moved them from one nipple to the other, and then down their torsos like probing giant stethoscopes, to their genitals.

'Now drop your trousers!'

She played the bells on her own breasts again and they watched mesmerised as they loosened their belts, unfastened buttons, slid down zips, and pushed both trousers and underpants to their knees. Two eager stiff cocks greeted her, their rosy glans smiling out from their foreskin sheaths.

Ella put down her bells and picked up the smallest two. They had small leather hoops which passed through a hole in the top of their handles, so they could be hung from their hooks on the tower wall. Now she hung them from the two cocks, finding a point of balance, about half way along, at which they held the cocks down horizontal.

'Youngest first,' she said, with a smile which made him want to please her oh so much. Standing only inches from him she unfastened the tight bodice of her dress from the rear, pulled her arms out of their short puffy sleeves, and let the front drop away from her breasts and fall to her waist. His cock lurched upwards and rang his bell.

'Ah, sweet music,' Ella whispered encouragingly. She lifted her own bell and eased the cold bronze metal down over the soft white flesh of her naked breast. Again the little bell rang. She slowly twisted her bell, and then moved it round in small circles, her breast inside it. And two bells rang! She turned halfway round to face the teacher. Now she was straight on to the distant tower, and the watching binoculars, the teacher's face inches to the left of her left breast, the nephew's just to the right of the other.

'But we must keep ringing the changes,' Ella said, dropping her hand-bells. 'Now my tits are my bells, and you're going to take their handles in your mouths and ring them for me.' She leaned forward slightly, easing her breasts apart with her hands until each nipple was taken by a mouth.

'Shake me! Suck me!' And the little bells below tinkled in resonance.

As the men went on sucking, Ella's hands searched out their balls. She cupped them in her palms and the bells rang. She probed behind the balls, pressing with her fingers, and the bells rang again.

Then Ella stepped back a pace. She wanted to watch these bells at work, and she wanted pictures! As the two cocks rested silent, horizontal, she wriggled her hips and slid her dress down to her feet. As soon as her thatch of pubic hair became visible the younger dick bobbed up fifteen degrees and back, sounding its excitement. Ella kicked her dress to the side and stood before them completely naked. She picked up the largest bell and unfastened its leather loop with her teeth. Young dick bobbed and tinkled two or three times as the nephew feasted his eyes on her. When she had removed the thong she eased her lips down around the wooden handle in mimicry of fellatio. The older dick rang his approval. Then when it was thoroughly wet, Ella held open her labia with one hand and slid the bell handle into her vagina. The dicks played a medley! Ella gripped the handle with her vagina, put her hands on her head, and by rocking slightly back and forth, joined the music.

When the cocks stopped bobbing up and down she picked up her other bell and repeated the removal of the thong and the sensual wetting of the handle. Only the older cock anticipated what was coming, jerking up violently with excitement. Ella turned sideways to them and stood with her feet a yard apart to open her legs. She held the vaginal bell in place at the front as she thrust her bottom out behind and steered the second saliva-sodden handle between her cheeks towards her second welcoming aperture. One cock rang as the tip of the handle disappeared between the folds of ass. Another, as Ella groaned sensually at the approach to the hole. Again, as she eased her bowels down and open, to let it in, her face tight with concentration. And both together as she relaxed, the handle gliding snug in her asshole. Then she lost sight and sound of the little bells. There was too much music in her crotch, in her ass! She rocked, pressing her clitoris against the metal of the bell. She gyrated her hips, holding both metal cups in place, one splaying her bottom cheeks apart, the other hard against her mons, squashing her clit, rubbing it, rubbing it, until she was overtaken by a sudden unplanned climax, and let go of the bells, hugging her breasts tight to her chest as if in an attempt to stop it. For a moment there was total silence. Then she gasped at the power of her orgasm as wave after wave of convulsions streamed outwards from her crotch, forcing the two bells from her orifices and causing a loud clatter as they fell to the ground.

Ella followed them down, dropping on to her hands and knees. She pushed the little bell on the teacher's dick right down as far as it would go and then tugged him by it round to her bottom. 'Up my cunt!' she said. 'I want your dong up my cunt! I want your clanger inside me! Ring me! Bang on me! Strike me! Fuck me!' At the same time she grabbed the nephew's dick and pulled him round in front of her. She licked the tip of him, rolled her tongue round the rim of his glans, and then sucked him in between pursed lips. As the bigger cock slammed up inside her cunt, its bell tingling and tinkling against her labia with every thrust and its rim playing tickle and run with her engorged clitoris, she took more and more of the smaller cock into her mouth, reaching down the soft underside with her tongue to flick and ring its little bell.

Ah, sweet music, sweet playful music . . . And from these playful miniatures, as she rocked back for the cock at one end of her and forward for the cock at the other, she caught a sense again of the voluptuous swell of the great bells in the tower, their ringing like singing in the ear of the heavens. The teacher juddered to a symphonic climax, carrying her with his breathless arpeggios of ejaculation and last percussive ass-smacking slams to her own satisfied completion.

She let go of both cocks and collapsed on to the grass on her back, limbs spread-eagled, face to the sky.

Her own sexual ingenuity and passion had won over the little Georgey Porgey robot, Ella mused, but how could it take on the big one, the major opus of SMIPT? A sexual conspiracy which had duped an entire village! She watched a jet plane streaming silently across the skies. A satellite beaming down sexual energy from the heavens! Manipulated, coded, and sold for pieces of silver!

'Please, miss . . .'

Ella turned her head to the side. It was the nephew, his still erect penis in his hand.

'Please miss, I wondered if . . . I mean, I'm sort of left feeling . . .'

He hadn't come yet!

'Of course,' Ella said, pulling her legs up at the knees and opening them wide to invite him in. 'Be my guest . . .'

And as the youth slid his penis gratefully and enthusiastically into her vagina, Ella grasped the key. She had to find a way of using him, and his uncle, and her cricketer, if not the entire village cricket team, including the scorer, and the delectable Susan. She had to mobilise her forces!

10

ONE FLOWER MAKES NO GARLAND

'Now it's your turn.'

Despite himself, Goode blushed. 'You mean out there, in broad daylight, with you watching every move through binoculars?'

Ella nodded emphatically. 'Or my telephoto lens.'

Goode had been forced to accept the evidence of his eyes. There was undoubtedly something bizarre going on: something very unusual and extremely powerful. And testing it out for himself might prove as much fun as watching Ella had been. But he wasn't sure how much he'd like playing to an audience. And who would he play with?

As if in answer, Ella nudged him and pointed to the lychgate. Two women were heading for the church, carrying enormous bundles of flowers.

'It's like Piccadilly Circus,' Ella said. 'With us poised on top of it all like Eros with a sheath full of arrows.'

But it was the allusion to all the coming and going that triggered a memory in Goode.

'Of course,' he said, glancing at the date on his wristwatch. 'It's the village fête tomorrow. First the peal of bells, then decking out the church . . .'

'So what happens tomorrow?'

'It was on my list of English customs for you. There are lots of stalls and games, treasure hunts, Morris dancing, throwing wet sponges at someone in the stocks.'

Ella seemed lost in thought. 'When?' she asked. 'I mean what time of day?'

'Afternoon. Then most of the adults come back in the evening for a bit of a booze-up.'

'Brilliant.' She smiled with a sense of cunning and determination which was lost on Goode. To help him catch up she asked, 'Where?'

'On the green, of course.'

She gave him time to let the bravado, the sheer immensity of her fledgling plan, sink in. Then she said, 'Blas Carnel may be clever, but his cleverness is harnessed to a shrivelling, possessive greed. He has no true vision. And he underestimates the power and the passion of the individual. We'll recruit the whole village and fuck SMIPT to oblivion!'

Goode wanted to tell her that he found the little flush of freckles over the bridge of her nose indescribably sexy.

'But first,' she said, bringing all her attention back to the present. 'We need to test your mettle.' She laughed briefly to put him at his ease. 'Are you going to share your fantasy with me?'

'Certainly not!'

'Then I'll stay here while you go spy out the flower-girls in search of inspiration.'

Almost an hour later she saw Goode walking out on to the green. Two women walked rather uncertainly, she thought, a pace or two behind him. Twenty yards out he spoke to them, and they strolled a little quicker and more confidently. By the time they reached the dip one of them had taken his hand in hers and the other skipped ahead eagerly.

Ella made herself comfortable on the roof of the tower and reached for the binoculars.

It was like the cliché from so many Hollywood movies, Goode thought, where the female lead is a boring sexless drip until the hero takes off her glasses and she is transformed. As they walked on to the green, Jill and Jane had their glasses removed. By the time they reached the dip their eyes were well and truly opened, their hair was down, and they were waiting desperately for the hero's kiss.

Jane had run ahead and was now languishing on the grass, plucking the petals from a daisy with covetous deliberation: 'He loves me . . . he loves me not . . . he loves me . . .'

Goode sat Jill a little up the slope on the far side, to be sure that she would be visible from the top of the church tower. He started picking flowers himself, pushing their slender stems into her hair.

'Like all art,' he said, as he surrounded her pretty face with daisies, 'flower arranging involves technique and grace. But there must also be spontaneity.' He leaned into the centre of his canvas and kissed her on the lips. He sought out her tongue with his own, mingled deliciously, thrust deeper into her mouth, and then reluctantly withdrew.

'And the artist must exploit all the materials at his disposal . . .' He reached for Jane's hand and pulled her towards him, repeating the sensual kiss on *her* lips. '. . . Ever seeking a new and vital synthesis.' He hooked one arm round Jane and the other round Jill, pulling both towards him. He slipped his hands up to their necks and drew them into a three-way kiss. First their lips touched and then, following his lead, all three tongues. It was tentative, even clumsy, but intensely exciting.

'My gorgeous two centrepieces,' Goode said at last as he broke away. He asked Jane to make a daisy chain as he eased Jill down on her back on the slope. He pulled the bottom of her blouse out of the waistband of her skirt and slowly unfastened the buttons. He peeled the fabric away from her chest like double outer leaves, revealing two shapely cones like hidden pistils. He slid his hand underneath her to unfasten the matronly bra and tussled briefly to remove it as though clearing away the strangling undergrowth.

Free of their restraints, the young breasts kept much of their conical shape, thrusting up boldly from Jill's chest and shimmering with a rude whiteness. Goode reached for the length of daisy chain which Jane had made, slit the first stem with his thumbnail and threaded the last one through it to make a small loop. He placed the necklace of flowers round one of Jill's breasts and then leaned over to suck the central nipple into a stiff stamen of insistent sex.

Jane started at once on a necklace for the other breast.

Goode told her to crown and anoint the second monarch exactly as he had done the first. And then he loosened the waistband of the skirt, preparing to explore and expose the deeper mysteries of this complex and magnificent bloom.

He slid the skirt down over hips and bottom, dragging it slowly over the lily-white, snowdrop-tight flesh of Jill's lower abdomen and pausing at the first suggestion of pubic husk. He kissed the little knot of her navel with his lips and ran his tongue around the folds of flesh as he gently penetrated the tiny receptacle. Then he cast around for a large white clover head and set it in the navel like a giant dew-drop.

He eased the skirt down over long bare legs and off Jane's feet. Likewise her unflattering underwear. He unfastened buckles on sensible sandals and tossed them away. Then he arranged the four limbs in a distinctly non-sensible but exuberant and alluring pose and stood back to admire the progress of his handiwork.

He picked a bunch of vibrant pink clovers and slid them individually on long stems through the gaps between Jill's toes. He knelt between her legs and set a dozen tiny daisy-heads in her pubic hair. He eased open the lips of her labia and slid into her vagina the stems of white clover until he made a furrow of flowers the length of her slit, culminating with a single pink bloom at the top, just beneath her clitoris.

Jill had become a galaxy of sex and flowers. Goode stood above her, scattering loose daisies as he intoned: 'Sun . . . Moon . . . Stars . . . Sex!'

With their little sunbeam heads on thin stems, the daisies blazed a glorious trail and then splattered on Jill's body like spermatozoa.

Eventually Jane asked, 'What about me?'

Goode looked about him for a wider range of complementary material.

'Don't move, either of you,' he said. 'I'm just popping over to the edge of the green.'

But Jane did move. When Goode returned with an armful of pickings from the verge of the mown area, she was lying on her stomach beside Jill, naked and ready.

He started with a huge ripe head of meadowsweet. He

scrunched it over her back and buttocks, showering her skin with hundreds of tiny cream-coloured petals. Then with his hands flat he gave her a gravelly massage, grinding the petals into her skin, drenching them both in their sickly-rich scent. When he had finished he casually swept away the fragments with a broom made of three long stems of barley.

He spread her limbs wide apart and continued his sweeping movements with the ears of barley, trailing the long hairs up her tender inside arm, through the sweet vale of her shaven armpit, and down her silken white flank. Jane moaned at the exquisite torture of it. Jill was watching silently with big eyes.

Goode ran his barley across the soles of Jane's feet, over her calves, along the supremely soft flesh at the back of her knees, and up her inner thighs. Again and again, one stretched-out limb after another, he tormented and delighted her.

Then at last he changed his pattern, and holding the barley close to its head he ran it back and forth along the joint line at the top of her legs. He started in the small of her back, along the dip between her bottom cheeks, and then round the curve and up the tighter slit of her vulva as far as her position allowed. At first he merely traced his course with the tips of the ticklish hairs, then he swept deeper into the crevices. At last he pressed home so that the knobbly ears of the grain ground into the crease, bringing an agony of lustful grunts and groans from both Jane and the watching Jill.

Now Goode discarded the barley and reached for a tangle of convolvulus. He tied one end of a long strand loosely around Jane's neck like a collar, then pulled her hands together, stretched way up above her head, and bound her wrists with the other end. A large white flower dangled from the impromptu handcuffs like a price tag. A second long strand, with half a dozen of the bold, fanfaring flowers along its length, he tied around one ankle and wound in a spiral up the leg, across at the top, and down the other leg to tie at the other ankle. Jane squirmed uneasily as he pulled the narrow stem tight in mimicry of its natural habit.

The sensation as it dug into the flesh of her thighs hovered between pain and pleasure but the pleasure principle carried her, wrapped as it was in such thrills of anticipation and deep promise.

Jill was deathly silent, as if she feared a reminder of her presence would inhibit them. But her lips were subconsciously mouthing encouragement: 'Yes! . . . Tighter! . . . Yes . . . Make it dig deeper!'

As Jill fervently hoped, Goode's attention swung back to Jane's bare bottom. He stripped the side shoots from a tough stem of bracken to make a switch. He flowered the flesh of Jane's cheeks with a dozen pin pricks from the jagged tip and then using the full length of the stem began to lash the expanse of creamy white bottom.

Jane whimpered at first. Jill's breathing suddenly imposed itself, heavy and involved. Goode looked up in time to see his bedrock of pretty daisies tremble uncontrollably – she had a hand pressed against her clover furrow – and then relax profoundly.

Jane took strength from Jill's climax, like the finely balanced spurt and bloom of different flora which follow on one after another in the same intimate space. She began hugging the earth with her crotch and begging for more of the bracken. She was deriving rich sexual nourishment from the arrangement. She wanted the bracken on her bottom harder, firmer, more resolutely. She pushed her bottom up to receive it. And Goode obliged her, crisscrossing her cheeks with an array of thin red lines which diffused rapidly to a general rosy glow until her bottom rose in a final begging heave and the lash came down on a shivering collapsing mound, her outstretched limbs now embracing the grass beneath them with relief and contentment.

Goode waited patiently while his little tutorial group came to order. And then he said, 'Just two charming variants, two adorable tableaux, two wonderful playlets at the meeting of Flora and Eros.'

Jane rolled over on to her back and smiled at him cheekily. 'And now *we* get to practise *our* arrangements on *you*!'

She jerked her wrists apart and broke her bonds menacingly.

'You did coax us out here,' Jill said very reasonably, 'with the promise of showing us some blooms we've never seen before. And everything you've produced so far is quite familiar, even if the arrangements are rather novel.'

'So out with it,' Jane insisted. 'Out with your willy.'

Jill nodded her agreement. 'I bet we've never seen one like it before.'

Goode gazed off into the distance and both women feared for a moment that he was contemplating escape. Both were determined to thwart him. But he knew far better than they that there was no way out, and he resigned himself to whatever fragments of his enabling fantasy they chose to pick up and act out. He undressed like a gentleman, trousers first.

They took turns playing with him. They cuddled his balls, stroked his bottom, pinched him playfully here and there, but above all they held his cock. They held it like a magnificent bloom, feasting their eyes; they brought it close to their faces and almost swooned with its intoxicating scent; they moved it right and left, up and down, admiring its various profiles. They held it tenderly, like a fledgling bird fallen from its nest; they held it hungrily, like a slice of watermelon. They beheld Goode's cock as a wonder of nature, with appreciation and a sense of awe. But it was also clearly to be used for their own and each other's pleasure: not a rare wild plant, but their own cut bloom.

When Jill got the idea of stroking the stem slowly up and down, Jane said, 'See how it surges upwards. I think it grows even bigger!'

Goode stood planted with his feet a little apart, face to the heavens like a sunflower.

Jill said, 'It's so shiny on the end. I think I want to suck it.'

Jane said, 'Feel how small the balls have shrunk.' She licked and kissed them, while Jill sucked the knoblike head.

Goode felt four hands and two mouths playing with his genitals and liked it. He liked it plenty. What a pity, he thought, that his bloom would wilt so soon. He said wistfully, 'A zoologist once observed a lion copulate a hundred and sixty times in two days.'

'But he's no lion,' Jill told Jane.

'And we don't have two days,' Jane told Jill.

'So I'm going to lie down here, and I want you to lie on top of me, George, and acquaint your darling willy with my fanny.'

Daisies and clover lay down on her back and George did as he was told. As soon as he was inside Jill, Jane climbed on top of him. The convolvulus around her legs rubbed against his, and her collar draped loosely over his shoulders. He could feel her thatch of pubic hair against his bare bottom. He was squashing clover heads with his cock and loose daisies slithered between his chest and the breasts below him. The meadowsweet flooded them all with its fragrance. And they made love.

Just as Goode approached his point of no return, Jill called time.

'Your turn, Jane.'

The setting changed, the bits and pieces of flower tatty and sweat-drenched. Jane was on her back on the ground, with George face down on top of her, but instead of lying sandwich like on top of him, Jill stayed on her feet, straddling his bottom so that he alternately thrust deep into Jane and then came up and slammed against Jill's vulva with his buttocks.

He came close to losing control again.

'Stop!' Jane said, rolling free beneath him. 'Let's make some proper triangles.' She lay Jill down again, on her back. 'You slide your willy in her cunny again, George, but lie at a bit of an angle. I'll make the third side and suck on Jill's pretty titties and you can say hello to my cunny and suck my little button.'

It was all so cooperative and sensible. And the rawness of it was strangely honed by the old-fashioned, matter-of-fact language. He felt rather like an expensive curio in the hands of two capable stalwarts who knew exactly how they wanted to run their jumble sale.

'Now I'll suck on Jane's clitty,' Jill said. 'And you suck

on my clitty, George. And put your peter in Jane's mouth so she can suck on it.'

'Now I'll sit on Jill's face so she can lick me out, and you kneel between her legs and roger her cunny with your willy, George, and if I lean forward a bit you can suck my titties at the same time.'

'Let's put him on his back and we'll kneel one over his willy and one over his tongue and watch the fun!'

Their timing was perfect. At every setting they took Goode right to the brink, but they never let him fall and wilt. He began to think the lion had it easy.

And then following a particularly athletic configuration Jill remarked that they had fucked themselves free of the last daisy, the last clover head, and the last fragment of convolvulus. With an intuitive consensus they created their final tableau.

Jane lay on her back with her arms stretched out above her head and opened her legs just sufficiently to allow Jill between them, lying face down. 'I'll be the engine,' Jane said. 'You get coupled at both ends, Jill, and I get to drive.'

The arrangement obviously suited.

'Start sucking my cunny,' Jane said. And Jill set to work with enthusiasm. 'Keep your body in a straight line with mine. That's good. I get to watch. I'm the driver. Now bring your knees up under you, to lift your bottom. Good. Spread your knees apart a foot or so and arch your back to show your cunny. That's it. Now George, come up behind her on your knees and slide your willy up her cunny. All in a straight line, and I'm the driver!'

And as soon as Jane had put her train together she started to move. Her language became cruder, its rawness like fuel to her motion.

'Stick it in me, Jill . . . all your tongue . . . up my cunt! That's good . . . lick me . . . suck me . . . eat my cunt!' She watched, and thrust her pelvis down on Jill's face. Then she looked down at the brow of Jill's bottom, and watched the shaft of Goode's penis appear and disappear below. 'Fuck her Georgey! Fill her cunt! Wham your cock up her! In and out, fuck fuck fuck . . . slap your belly against her bum!'

Goode had time to wonder if these two had something going between them already. He had heard of explosive hen parties in the provinces, with a compliant man as a catalyst. But this was something in another realm! These two women had been as dry as the desert, and now . . . the deluge . . . the great flood . . . and how they were enjoying it!

'Suck the clit! Yes! With your chin up my cunt!' Jane strained her head to watch Jill do as she was told. 'Push your chin in! Further! Further in! Fill me up . . . Split me open!' She bore down. She rocked her pelvis up and down rapidly. 'Suck my clit!' She grabbed Jill's head with her hands and pushed it further into her vulva and rubbed herself furiously against it. Then she looked down at Jill's bottom. 'Fuck her! Fuck her cunt! Fuck her bum! Suck me! Sex! Sex! Cock! Cunt! I'm coming! I'm spending! Lick me! Lick me!' And with a final screech, still hugging Jill's head to her crotch, her whole torso lifted off the earth, her back arched to meet the terrific vaginal contraction, and the back of her head and her heels jammed hard against the ground as she shuddered against the invisible wall, the sound barrier of her orgasm. But like a wave passing down a train, the shudder and jolting passed on to Jill. She jerked her head backwards. Her breasts heaved and fell, and she hugged the earth with her chest as her entire womb seemed to be sucked up inside her. Her pelvis jerked forward with her own contractions. Her bottom shook, splayed backwards . . . and then Goode collapsed forward around it in the third swiftly consecutive orgasm. He imagined his cock had sprung free of him and was hurtling forward in the slipstream of Jill's tremors, right along the line in search of Jane's. In truth it was his sperm, shooting forth from him hot and fast. Sperm for Jill and sperm for Jane, it sped from him with frightening vigour and such a splendid and appreciative sense of occasion.

Ella was still watching the green through binoculars when Goode climbed up on to the roof of the tower twenty minutes later. She greeted him in a tone of muted congratulation.

'Not bad, Mr Goode. You gave a whole new meaning to the concept of a multiple pile-up.'

Goode paused in cool acceptance of her praise and then asked if they had left a burnt patch on the grass.

'I'm looking out for SMIPT,' she answered. 'They've got some sort of machine for measuring their uptake of energy from the village, and whenever I've had fun and games on the green before, it's upset their takings. I had a feeling that I blew the machine's fuse when I escaped from Pod Manor, but they might have mended it by now.'

'And my little multiple pile-up might have set red lights flashing?'

'Something like that.' And then she smiled briefly. 'You really were rather exciting to watch.'

Goode suddenly reached for her hand and pulled her to her feet. 'Come on, let's go to the hide for the night, while the coast is still clear.'

Ella considered the idea and quickly agreed. It dovetailed nicely with her plans and in the lull before the storm it might be nice to snuggle somewhere a little more cosy.

Goode left her in the shadow of the lychgate while he slipped over to the King's Arms to buy two enormous cold-beef sandwiches and a couple of bottles of Guinness. Then they retraced their steps cross-country, pausing now and then to make sure they weren't being followed, and went to earth in the nature-hide.

It had been a scorching hot afternoon and now a dense, slow-moving bank of cloud had drifted low over the sky, trapping the heat of the day in a stifling fug. They sat on the rough wooden floor of the hide with their heads below the parapet and whispered tales of their lives in London and New York. They ate their body-strengthening meal. And then they whispered some more. They both knew that an early night would be body-strengthening too. But instead they kissed. They kissed long, on the lips. Eventually one of them whispered that making love was also body-strengthening. They kissed some more. Then one of them said it was lovely sometimes to have sex without penetration of any kind. And then they undressed.

They spread their clothes across the log floor and lay

down on top of them. Ella kissed Goode's face, all of his face. And with infinite tenderness Goode's hands roamed her back, her sides, her chest. They curled up. Goode kissed Ella's feet, every inch, every molecule of her feet; and Ella touched his skin, any part of his skin, with a touch as aware as breath. They moved again. They purred. And after a tireless, infatuated hour they could no longer tell which hands were theirs, which lips their own, or where in this supremely sexual touch lay the border between the different bodies; so that two became as one, each lost themselves, and the spirit in which they moved became one of blissful, endless orgasm.

They made love deep into the night . . . and beyond, so that one of them would wake up in the early hours, with the chorus of birdsong at first light, or in the eerie stirrings of a woodland dawn, and feel the other body warm and sleeping beside, and half mixed up still, and the creation of their sex together lay over them like an embroidered quilt.

11

FÊTEFUL AMBITION

As Ella scrutinised the unfolding scene through her telephoto lens, Goode tried to follow her vision through his binoculars.

'Ah,' Ella sighed with relish. 'The promise of sex. Sex in the offing. Sex on the wind!'

Goode scanned the green anxiously. Was there something he was missing?

'The merest hint of sex, just a smell of it, is so heavenly to me,' she whispered. 'I want to dive into it, swim in it, wade in it. Anything with so much as the whiff of sex simply knocks me over.'

Goode passed over the most pacific tug o' war he had ever seen and tracked the line of stalls beyond it, sniffing in vain for a scent of sex.

'It's in here,' Ella said, tapping her temple with the fingers of one hand while still holding the telephoto to her eye with the other. 'And it's up to us to lay down our fantasies like a sexual minefield.'

Goode was raring to go. The momentous day had begun late, sheltered as they had been by the woodland canopy from the rising sun. Ella had insisted they walk from the hide back to the car and drive into Pod Magna, where they had demolished a magnificent English breakfast at the Station Inn. Then she had commandeered his credit cards and leisurely taken him shopping for clothes.

Ella spent half an hour in and out of a changing cubicle choosing the right pair of blue jeans. She insisted Goode discard his underwear, and stroked his balls and bottom into the perfect fit. Then she asked for a pair of scissors and cut the legs off mid-thigh. For herself: a denim skirt similarly mid-thigh, tight but manoeuvrable, sans knickers. She fitted them both out in sleeveless white cotton shirts which buttoned up the front, so they could be worn open to expose chest and breast. And for maximum exposure of flesh she bought them white canvas slip-on deck shoes with navy blue trim. As an afterthought she added baggy Fair Isle sweaters in case it turned cool in the evening. They looked like a pair of Nordic Love Gods, raised in the Aegean.

After the shops Ella had taken Goode to the SMIPT yard, where he had diverted the girl in the shopfront while she went about her business round back. And from there to the more traditional firm of Alfred Higgins and Son. She needed help, she insisted, and Son of Alfred had bargained hard. Ella had been obliged to reward him with an invitation to the time of his life. But she was wary of outsiders on the green. She felt he needed a chaperone whose sexuality she could depend on. She rang Toni.

At last Ella felt happy that all the pieces were falling into place and they had returned to the hide, and from there, with a furtiveness which slowed them to a crawl, to their advance HQ atop the church tower. Now at last events were accelerating and Ella's lieutenant listened eagerly to his briefing.

'We're going to lay down our fantasies like mines, to be triggered later, when we move on to the green this evening.'

Goode nodded attentively.

'We've got to keep the fantasies loose and fluid. Couples can stay just with each other if they want to. And there's to be no compulsion about anything. It's all to be generous, open, joyful . . . but as over the top as people want to go. All the little sexual imps and faeries from deep down inside men *and* women can come up and play, and explore, and have a good time. We are the enablers, and we're making up for an awful amount of lost time, remember. We've got to release so much pent-up lustful glorious sexual energy that we beam up more than Blas Carnel ever in his wildest dreams imagined an English village capable of. This orgy of sex has got to be so energetic we burn up his satellite and knock it out of orbit forever!'

Goode wanted to show that he had got the idea, and looked through his binoculars again. Dog owners were parading their pets round a show court. 'We could have a nude parade for exhibitionists, with prizes for the biggest cock and the biggest tits.' And then thinking he hadn't got off to a frightfully original start, he added, 'and if anyone was into it, masters and mistresses could lead round their sexual slaves wearing collars, like dogs.'

'We'll need a Queen of the Carnival,' Ella said. 'To give the prizes.'

'How about Toni?'

Ella dug him in the ribs with her elbow and put up her own candidate: 'Susan.'

'We'll have a whole string of games for exhibitionists. A competition for strippers and one for wankers; first round all male and second all female. Then games for pairs: best cock-sucker, best cunt-licker, best fuckers.'

'But not competitions, just games,' Ella said. 'With a prize for every entrant. Someone could hand out flowers, and tape them to chests like medals, until you'd earned enough to make a garland.'

'What about side-stalls?' Goode asked. 'They've got a feely box over there, with weird things inside you've got to guess by touch. We could have a feely stall for the lovers of anonymity. They stand hidden with their vulva or penis up to the hand hole and anyone who comes along can feel them up.'

'You could put your bum up to it, too, if you wanted to give people a bit of a surprise.'

Goode laughed. 'And if you wanted to give them a bit of a surprise back, you could feel with a different digit, instead of your fingers.'

Ella observed the hoop-la stall briefly and then described her fantasy version: 'This one's for women. You pay for your three hoops by sucking one of the stallkeeper's cocks into a good big stiffy. The schoolteacher and his nephew would run this one very well. Once they're sucked good and big they step back five paces from the barrier and face the woman. She has to get her hoops on to his cock. If she succeeds, he lies down on his back and she gets to ride him. For every hoop on his cock she gets ten humps with her cunt on it.'

Goode followed suit with the darts stall: 'This is for the men. Maybe Jane and Jill would like to run it. Your three darts come with a little sucker attached on the end, from the toy arrows in the Robin Hood prizes, and you pay for them by thoroughly licking the bottom cheeks of one of the delectable stallkeepers. She walks five paces from the barrier, facing away from you, and you lick the end of your little arrow and aim for her bottom. If you manage to stick one on her, you get to cross the barrier and reclaim it. She bends over and you get to stick your very own big arrow in her from behind. Ten thrusts in her vagina for each arrow you stuck on her bottom.'

'What's the marquee with the slatted wooden floor for?' Ella asked.

'It's the beer tent.'

'Great. We won't need any beer tonight. It can be for watersports. We're sure to find some voyeur from the well-dressing committee to organise it. If you want to join in you write down your preference on a piece of paper: you like to wet yourself while someone watches; you like to lie under a pisser, male or female specified; you want to spray someone; you like an audience, or not; you just want to watch. The organiser gives you a number like at a busy café. Then as time goes on you listen to the loudspeaker. He hoses down the last lot and then announces: "Numbers twelve and fifteen to the water-sports tent, please!" '

Then the morris dancers started their act and Goode the wordsmith launched into the history of the dances. Ella was surprised to hear that most of them grew out of fertility rites, celebrating the revival after death of pagan gods just as spring and summer bring renewal to the earth after winter.

'Let's have them on chairs,' she said decisively, 'where they can't tread on anyone's toes. They sit naked on chairs formed into a big circle, facing outwards. They can keep the bells round their calves if they want. Then the women dance round them in a big circle. It's like musical chairs. When the fiddler stops playing they jump on to the nearest cock and fuck it until the music starts again. When a cock hurries from summer into winter that cock goes into the middle, where the Maid Marian character tries her best to renew it, either with her mouth or her riding crop.'

That put her in mind of her gangly scorekeeper who had enjoyed the novel beatings of the bounds so much and she began to weave a playful fantasy for the lovers of slippers, canes, whips, thongs, collars, handcuffs, stocks . . .

'The stocks!' she said. She watched through her long-distance lens. The village policeman had his face and hands locked in the old village stocks at the far end. Punters were paying ten pence to charity for a wet sponge to throw at him.

'If Blas Carnel were here,' Ella said, 'that would be the place. And he would be the one participant denied the freedom of consent. He would be forced to watch it all. And perhaps he could even repay a little of what he has robbed. We could have a platform and the punters would queue for a turn to climb up and present his captive face with their request. A cunt in need of sucking, perhaps, or a cock, or . . .'

Goode said, 'And we could have someone into heavy spanking stationed behind, to ensure his wholehearted commitment to his task.' He had just spotted Ted the Village Stores and thought he would execute the task admirably.

As the afternoon wore on, they concentrated on more basic images of fucking. They pictured orgasm after orgasm. Until finally they thought simply of flesh. Naked male and female flesh . . . and the merest scent of sex.

Ella reached for a bottle of lotion, and in the lowering rays of the sun began to rub it into her long bare legs, and then Goode's, like a coach readying her players for the big game.

In Goode's Thamesside apartment, his sister's three chums were up and ready for the adventure of the new night a little earlier than usual.

It had been a peculiar couple of days, and thinking back over events, Melissa was not at all sure she had had her fair share of the action; Lallie was damned sure she wasn't going to get elbowed into third place yet again; and Fiona was still haunted by the image of the battered joker in the Indian outfit who had stolen Goode from her before he had delivered the big sausage.

It had been a sultry night in the clubs after Goode disappeared. The three of them stuck together in hopes that they would find him, and they lubricated their fractious companionship with too much alcohol. When they slunk home at three o'clock, sexually frustrated and as catty as ever, none of them noticed the flash Cadillac parked on the opposite side of the street.

Blas Carnel was very happy to see them tripping up the steps of the condominium. He was happy his orgone capacitors and transmitters were back in working order. He was happy that the TV ads he was associated with were giving him such a hard-on. And he was happy at the thought of the billions of dollars which would soon be lined up behind him. He was so happy that his handling of this final loose end might almost be described as complacent.

He flicked a switch on his armrest and spoke to his Head of Security, who was behind the wheel, and Head of Personnel beside him: 'The girl I want will be along soon now, boys. So you go on up there and get yourselves inside so you can be ready and waiting for her. Keep those three out of the way and above all quiet, and whatever you do, no goddamn cock-ups.'

So the two heavies stole into the building five minutes after the chums and sneaked their way to the door of Goode's flat. It was unlocked and they entered stealthily.

Fiona was not unused to attractive men stealthily entering and departing from apartments in the early hours, and her immediate reaction was one of envy of her two companions. Melissa and Lallie had made straight for their rooms, but Fiona had stripped off her clothes in the kitchen lounge and had just slipped her naked feet into her fluffy highheeled mules to traverse the stretch of linoleum which stood between her and the coffee-maker. As the door opened she reached casually for her ankle-length kaftan, more in regard for their sense of modesty than her own.

And then they were on her. She struggled briefly, but

she was balanced precariously on the high heels, and her arms were encumbered half-in and half-out of the kaftan's sleeves. So she used her mouth, and cursed them heartily. One of the men grabbed her from the front and clamped his hand over her lower face, the lapels of his suit pressing against her naked breasts. The kaftan slipped to the floor, but the other man grabbed her arms from behind. He'd picked up one of the nylon stockings she had so recently stripped off, and tied her wrists together behind her back. She tried to bite the fingers over her mouth and scream, but the man in front stuffed something into her mouth to stifle the noise. It was her bra. He'd stuffed her bra into her mouth to gag her and now the man behind was fastening it in place with her suspender belt. She squirmed and felt herself squashed, bound and gagged, with the suit of the second man rubbing hard against her naked bottom.

'We're not going to hurt you,' he said. 'Just cooperate and you'll come to no harm.'

The voice reassured her despite all common sense. It had the bloated tone of a poseur, its menace a theatrical pretence.

Her breasts bounced uncomfortably as she was pushed down on to a straight-backed chair to which her arms were strapped tightly using her other nylon stocking.

'Maybe the noise scared away the target,' one of the men said. 'I'd better check back to the street.'

Soon after he left, Melissa stumbled bleary-eyed from her room asking if there was any coffee.

Fiona made a muffled groan and strained against her bonds, her thighs and her breasts wresting awkwardly.

'Well, well, well . . . holding out against our friends are we darling?'

Fiona tried to shout a warning with her eyes, but Melissa just took it as a selfish 'hands off'. Then the man grabbed her and tried to stuff Fiona's knickers in her mouth.

'Ah, but that's not my game, Billy-boy. I like to be the bossy one in bed.' And in three lightning moves which left him stunned she jerked his buttoned-up jacket down off his shoulders, trapping his arms; pushed his trousers down to his knees, restraining his legs; and jammed Fiona's freshly doffed frilly pink knickers into *his* mouth.

The man struggled rather feebly, she thought. And his cock stood out as stiff as a signpost.

'So you like it this way too?' Melissa laughed, enjoying her humiliation of Fiona's strongman and following it through to a thorough conclusion. She whipped a length of cord out of a blind and bound his hands together. She pushed him backwards over her leg so he fell to the floor and she quickly secured his hands to a radiator leg. She twisted him on to his back, pushed his trousers down to his ankles, and tied his feet to a pipe on the other side of the room. He was absolutely secure, and she flicked his stiff cock in Fiona's sight as a sign of conquest.

But he was still making too much noise. She cast around for Fiona's satin camisole. Then she hitched up the long cotton T-shirt which she wore to bed and squatted with her naked crotch over his chest to tie the camisole around his head and hold the knickers firmly in his mouth.

She neither saw nor heard the second man. He came back just as she had lowered herself on to her captive's cock and she screamed with dismay as this newcomer tried to pull her off it. The man was single-mindedly concerned with his boss's insistence on silence. But Fiona's lingerie was all used up! In desperation he reached down and ripped Melissa's thin shift from top to bottom. He tore at it furiously, then swiftly thrust a chunk of one piece into her mouth, and tied the other round her head to complete the gag. Then with one hand round her chest to pin her arms and keep her pinioned on his colleague's cock, with his other hand he unhooked his own braces and tugged them down off his shoulders under his jacket. He tied her hands together behind her back with one end, pulled her feet up close to her bottom, and bound them together with the other end. She rolled off the cock and lay on her side on the floor, naked with her knees bent behind her, flush with a thwarted excitement. Fiona, too, was finding it all rather thrilling, despite herself, and couldn't resist rubbing her naked crotch back and forth against the polished wood of the seat she found herself so intimately bound to.

And then Lallie, who had crashed on her bed fully clothed the minute she came in, woke up. Whether stirred by the thumping reverberations of sundry limbs hitting the floor or by the nascent sexual whirlpool in the room nearby, curiosity drew her out. And her first reaction was anger.

'You greedy scheming bastards! Leave me out again, would you?'

The place was teeming with lurid sex – Fiona and Melissa bound and hot, and the cock on the floor – and it fuelled all her paranoia as the shorty with the big tits. But she would show them!

'Shh! Shh . . .' Head of Personnel was also paranoid, but about the noise. Things were going hopelessly wrong. He felt he had to make a stand on the noise. If only he could keep things quiet!

'Shh! Shh . . .' Lallie mimicked, twice as loud.

'Please!' he begged in a desperate whisper. 'Anything but noise.' He was blinded by fear – fear of his boss or fear of this Amazon – or maybe by sex, and he hung on to this one achievement like a lifesaver.

'Then crawl over here on your knees, buddy-boy, and take off my knickers, or I'll scream the house down.'

He scrambled to obey, his braceless trousers gradually slipping down and his giveaway cock thrusting despite himself through the fly of his boxer shorts. When he reached her feet he pulled up her crumpled skirt. She was wearing black silk knickers with lots of lace, and black seamed nylons held up by pink garters. The man slid her knickers down over her thighs to the ground. He was trembling, mesmerised, and entirely in her control. She stepped out of the knickers and held out her hand for them.

'Now open your mouth.'

She stuffed her knickers in.

'And now the stockings.'

Muted, he pulled down the garters and rolled down her black stockings. She stepped out of them. By now a wet lacy hem of her knickers had slipped out of his mouth. She stuffed it back in and stretched the two elastic garters round his head to keep the gag in place. Then she ordered him on to the floor on his back, alongside his mate, and using her nylons she tied his hands above his head to the other leg of the radiator, and his feet to the same pipe opposite. She executed a nice neat reef knot and clapped her hands for the good old Girl Guides. Then she stripped off the rest of her clothes.

'Now it's Lallie's turn to play,' Lallie said delightedly. '*Precious things come in little parcels* and *last but not least*.'

She toured the room, fondling her own body narcissistically, followed in total silence by four pairs of eyes.

She leaned over Melissa, deliberately thrusting her bottom in front of Fiona's face, and played with her friend's breasts dismissively, as if in judgement of their size and enjoying the fealty of their stimulated, engorged nipples. Then she turned, arse down over Melissa's face, and slid her middle finger along the wooden seat between Fiona's thighs and up her vagina. It was deliciously slippery.

Reassured that the girls would enjoy the show, Lallie turned to the men. She pulled back their ruffled clothing to expose more flesh and then she prodded, poked and tickled them into a frenzy of impotent squirms. She slithered her own wet vulva up and down one limb after another and at last settled it on a face, and took one big cock in one hand and one in the other. She called them Bill and Ben and as she stroked them up and down she talked to them like finger puppets.

With her vulva slithering up and down from Bill's nose to his chin, she took Ben in her mouth and sucked. Then she forced her vulva down on to Ben's chin, her labia spreading to envelop it, while she stroked Big Ben up and down with her hand and took Bill into her mouth. At last she crouched above Big Ben and opening her labia with her fingers, lowered her cunt on to him. She poked at Bill and when he wriggled away from her she went down on his cock with her mouth. So she sucked and fucked at the same time. And when either Bill or Ben seemed like they were getting too selfishly preoccupied and threatened to be a spoilsport and spit at her, she slid off them both, and taunted them with her feet, and then rejoined play the other way round, with Ben in her mouth and Bill up her cunt.

In the car outside, Blas Carnel was getting impatient. It

was looking like the girl he wanted wasn't going to show. And by all the reports from his people over the phone, and the evidence of his dick in front of the TV, it no longer mattered.

'Go call them back, honey,' he told his squaw.

Five minutes later, when she hadn't returned, he got lonely and went after her. He didn't like being left alone. And he didn't like the dark. And he didn't like getting out on the wrong side of the road and he'd be damned pleased when this business was up and running and he could get back to the Big Country.

So when he opened the door on Goode's apartment, he found the scene instantly reassuring. He sat in a back corner unnoticed and watched.

His squaw was wrestling with a spirited little thing with gallon-sized dumplings up front, the girl as bare as a prairie and the squaw with her leather duds hanging off in tatters. Head of Personnel was flat on his back, gagged with black knickers and pink garters, tied up with nylon stockings. And Head of Security lay alongside, also tied, with pink panties and another piece of lingerie stuffed in his mouth. Both had stiff cocks under imminent attack. A gorgeous curly blonde was crouching over one of them, a white brassière hanging half out of her mouth, a black suspender belt round her head, and her hands tied round a kitchen chair which she bore on her back like a fetish. Another cunt was coming down on top of the other cock. She was slobbering round the edges of her gag with effort because her hands, which were tied behind her back, were connected to her feet, which were also tied behind her back, by some sort of elastic material, and every time she moved one there was a boing and it jerked the other. She kept coming off and then climbing back on, her cunt like a yo-yo.

He pulled out his cock and masturbated as he watched.

The two wrestlers got in a close arm hug and rolled over, knocking Yo-Yo off her cock, before coming to a panting rest between Bill and Ben. Something seemed to give between them, and when Squaw's jaw went down on Dumpling's dumpling it was suddenly not a bite, but a suck. Dumpling's thighs gripped around Squaw's thigh and pumped not in a squeeze, but a frig. Chair-back had got herself into a steady rhythm on Big Ben. And Yo-Yo had succeeded in mounting up again and though she toppled forward so her breasts squashed against Ben's face, and her feet caught Squaw in the crotch, she was managing to fuck Bill's cock with her cunt.

Carnel stood and walked to the edge of the fracas, still masturbating himself.

In a period of two or three minutes, Lallie rubbed herself to orgasm on the leather-wrapped thigh of Squaw, who was sucking her breasts; Ben shot his sperm up into Fiona, who juddered to a climax on top of him and then toppled sideways on to Bill; Bill jerked away and in a reflex reaction spewed his come into Melissa's cunt; Melissa strove with supreme athletic effort for her own orgasm, in the course of which her foot convulsed rapidly between the bottom cheeks of Squaw; and Squaw squealed as she spat out Lallie's breast and writhed in the midst of it all with her own orgasmic spasm.

There was a moment's rest and total silence.

And then Carnel's sperm shot forward from his own hand and sprayed over the heap of bound and gagged fuckers. They heard it splatter here and there on naked flesh.

Blas Carnel liked these three limey girls. He said they had spunk in them. The following night he took them out in style to see how they could cope with the social side of things. They coped very well. And so he put to them a proposition.

The following evening he was entertaining three American guests. One was the head of a religious broadcasting organisation, with whom he hoped to do much mutually beneficial business in the very near future. One was a congressional leader whose influence was vital to Carnel's new venture. And the third was a very highly positioned officer of law enforcement who constituted the ultimate in insurance policies. He needed a female companion for each of them. For dinner at his place in the country.

He would pick them up around three the following afternoon. They would have to rise a little earlier than usual.

12

INTERSTELLAR OVERDRIVE

Most people were still fully dressed when Blas Carnel and his party arrived on the green at Pod Parva rather late on the day of the village fête. A man in a boiler suit had torn holes in the linings of his pockets and was masturbating excitedly but relatively unobtrusively in the voluminous privacy of his clothing. A few other men and women were tentatively rubbing their genitals through their trousers and skirts.

Ella and Goode were circulating genially, their shirts casually unbuttoned and their tight-fitting denim shorts and skirt open at the waist revealing a V of naked abdomen down to a hint of pubic hair. They had just begun to weave their web, with a stroll round the perimeter and a few broad passes across the green to establish their irresistible sexual lays. With a tiny smiling gesture here and a little erotic suggestion there they probed and prodded at a few of their fantasies. They were both supremely confident. They could feel the magic at work at once, but the degree of sexual pleasure they were aiming to generate demanded patience and a slow unfolding. They needed passion which was prolonged and stretched, with variety and refinement, to the very highest intensity. They triggered the first detonator, a simple show. A little sexual parade. And then Ella spotted Blas Carnel.

She quickly located Susan and recruited her willing help. 'Steer him straight to the stocks. Tell him it's an old feudal custom – the lord of the manor has to face one wet sponge on carnival day. Tell him anything you like but whatever you do, don't flirt!'

Ella watched from a safe distance. Susan was superb! He

couldn't resist her. He put his hand on her ass. Don't respond! Don't let him feel you! Ella willed the little village maiden onwards. She was leading the big Texan with her tight little bottom . . . she was nearly there . . . But Ella heard a man behind her telling his wife to enter the show. She giggled about her breasts not being big enough, and he promised he'd suck them up for her. He was pulling her blouse out of her skirt to get at them . . . Hurry up Susan! Don't let him turn this way! . . . A man asked where he had to go to enter the big cock show. A woman standing nearby slid her hand down the front of his trousers. She said she'd tell him if he stood a chance . . . And then Carnel was there. He put his hands in the little scooped-out places on each side of the big hole in the middle of the beam, and turned round to savour the quaintness of it with his American guests. Ella dashed up in front of him and pulled his head forward and down by the chin-strap of his ten-gallon hat. Susan dropped the top bar across his neck and wrists. And Ella slid the locking pin in place, snapped the padlock shut, and withdrew the key. She smiled at the dumbfounded squaw beside her, reached a hand inside the belt of her tasselled leather miniskirt, and dropped the key into the crotch of her knickers.

'He's all yours, honey.'

Carnel watched three women parade past, thrusting their naked bosoms in front of them to appreciative applause, and he spluttered furiously: 'Get me outta here!'

But the squaw didn't move. At last she took a deep, long breath, and as she let it out she smiled. Ella's instinct had been right again, and she left the stocks assured that the villain of the piece would be well catered for.

The buxom exhibitionists strolled past the three chums and the VIPs they were chaperoning.

'So this is your quiet little retreat in the country.' Fiona had spotted Goode, who was keeping a furtive eye on them. 'I'm not surprised you always wanted to keep it to yourself!'

'Ah, well,' he smiled, coming forward. 'Good will out.' He shook hands with the bewildered visitors and then winked at Lallie. 'Why don't you enter?'

'Yes, go on,' Melissa said, aware that they were all three

outsiders and for once sounding genuinely supportive. 'Show these country bumpkins a pair of *real* boobs.'

There was a general chorus of approval for the idea, especially from the influential congressman who was holding Lallie's hand. The poor thing was taken aback at the simple sincerity of compliments from all sides, and blushed a very becoming bright red.

'She will if *you* enter the sausage show,' Fiona told Goode. 'You sort of owe it to us anyway.'

Goode agreed at once, and unzipped his fly there and then. His cock stood out magnificently, and a collective gasp of amazement escaped from the little crowd of admirers round him. Everyone wanted to touch it, as if to verify that it was real, and the high-ranking officer of law enforcement let his hand linger lovingly, stroking the skin up and down several times before reluctantly letting go when Fiona tugged just a mite possessively on his arm.

The ice was broken, and though these three sexual sophisticates in their short skirts, black nylons and shiny high heels stood out from the villagers in their floral frocks and sensible sandals, it was clear to Goode that they were one with them in spirit.

Lallie now had no choice but to unbutton her chemise and unhook her bra. Her breasts seemed to break loose and tremble with the thrill of freedom, their pink stiff nipples broadcasting her uncharacteristic shyness. The congressman carried her bra like a pageboy and joined the parade a respectful pace behind his liege-lady.

Fiona's lawman had spotted the big cocks all lining up together and dragged her over to help in the judging. And Melissa's religious broadcaster got the idea there was something very exciting going on over at the marquee, and insisted they check it out.

But there was another pair of nylons and shiny high-heeled shoes. These were bright red, and the stockings fishnet. Goode had spotted them through a throng of legs gathering for the cock-sucking show. He bent low to the ground and followed the classic line of fishnetted ankle, calf, knee, and thigh to the hem of a short, tight skirt in scarlet PVC. He worked his way forward. And then he heard a familiar voice, at once alluring but assertive, seductive but empowering.

'Not cocksucking, handsome – fellatio! I promise you: it will be the treat of a lifetime.'

The voice, and the memory, sent a tingle up Goode's spine. He worked his way round until he was standing next to the drainage man, Son of Higgins, from Pod Magna.

'She's absolutely right,' he whispered in the man's ear, just loud enough for Toni to hear. 'You'd be a fool not to take her up on it.' Then he and Toni kissed affectionately, cheek to cheek and then back again, like the French, and Goode melted away into the crowd.

The games were rolling fast and free.

Ella started the hoop-la herself. She grabbed Susan and together they searched for the schoolmaster and his nephew. They found them in the wanking show, picking up some new techniques from the morris men, and dragged them over to the side-stall. They took off the rest of their clothes and then knelt before them, Susan taking the younger, thinner cock in her mouth, and Ella the uncle's. When they were good and stiff they stood the men at the back of the stall, facing forwards, and carried their three hoops to the barrier.

Their first shots went wild. The second time their hoops both hit the cocks, but fell to the floor.

'It's not fair,' Ella said. 'Mine's too thick!'

'At least yours is sticking out,' Susan said. 'Mine's so energetic it's almost flush with his stomach.'

But by the third try the men had got the idea, and two good aims together with two cooperatively moving targets achieved success.

'On your backs on the ground!' Ella squealed with delight. She and Susan ducked under the barrier and went to claim their prize. They pulled up their skirts and tucked them in their waistbands, and knelt beside each other above their men's cocks. Then with one hand grasping their respective targets and the other holding open their labia, they lowered themselves into place. They fidgeted briefly to get comfortable. Then they held hands with each other and fucked.

'All right! All right! You've had your turn!'

There was a queue of eager women waiting at the barrier.

'Ten frigs per hoop, that's only fair!'

Susan and Ella stood and dropped their skirts. A naked woman carrying an enormous bundle of flowers in the crook of her arm rushed forward to tell them they'd done very well, and more than earned their first flower. She pushed the stem of a huge marigold into Ella's hair, and another into Susan's waistband.

Then Susan froze momentarily as a voice announced over a loudspeaker: 'Numbers five and nine to the water-sports tent, please.'

Her excitement got the better of her embarrassment and she bobbed up and down with a nervous thrill, holding on to Ella's arm. 'That's me! Oh, it's me!'

Ella smiled reassuringly.

'Do you want to come with me?' Susan asked her. 'I'm sure it would be OK.'

'I'll take a rain check,' Ella answered, pushing her sweet protégé in the direction of the marquee.

And so she moved on, she and Goode mingling with the crowd like hosts at a party, introducing like-minded guests, and occasionally lively opposites; probing for common interests and sparking new overtures; staying just long enough to make a newcomer welcome, or to lubricate some new social conjunction. Except that every dalliance was an erotic one, and the medium of exchange was always sex.

When Goode next bumped into Lallie she was wearing a deep blue basque with suspenders attached to hold up her stockings. Her proud breasts spilled free over the top of the basque, and her surprisingly petite bottom and motte were naked below it. 'He begged it off someone for me,' she said, nodding dismissively at the ground behind her.

At the end of the dog lead which she jerked aggressively from time to time was her congressman. Round his neck he wore a leather collar to which the lead was fastened, but the rest of him was naked. He crawled behind her on his hands and knees, his cock so stiff it tried to bury itself in his navel.

'Lick my shoes, my little doggy-woggy!' she said for Goode's amusement.

The man bent to her feet and licked the stiletto heels of her shiny black shoes, his bottom wagging from side to side in sheer bliss.

'You can ease up on your chaperone role if you want to,' Goode told her.

She smiled angelically. 'No way. He's far too rich and powerful to let out of my sight.'

Meanwhile at the water-sports tent, Susan and the adolescent scorekeeper had been ushered into the play area by a matronly coordinator who assured them that there would be no spectators, as this had been their mutual request.

They were quivering with nervous anticipation, exaggerated by shyness, and neither spoke nor looked at each other. As though for something to do with her hands, Susan tugged off her little pixie boots and stood them neatly on the side. That set the boy going, and he started undressing. He was so nervous he whipped his clothes off in no time, and then had to stand and watch, his hands crossed over his genitals, while Susan peeled off her white cotton socks, unbuttoned her blouse, and stepped out of her skirt. When she was naked at last she said, faintly: 'Well, I suppose I'd better lie down underneath you, since that's what I wrote on my form.'

'Yes, I suppose you better had,' he answered.

She sat down on the wooden slatted floor and stretched out her feet towards him. He spread his legs apart and she wriggled down on her back until her genitals were directly underneath his. She looked up at him and said, 'Right.'

'Right,' he said back.

'Do what you wrote down you wanted to do, then. It's what I want, too.'

'Right.'

'You'll have to take your hands away.'

'Right.' And he did so.

But Susan was puzzled. She couldn't understand how he was going to pee down on her stomach and chest when his penis was pointing up at his own stomach and chest. The boy was obviously too mortified to think about such finer details. His face strained and he grunted with effort. Then he said, 'I can't piss when I've got a hard-on.'

Susan felt for him. She stroked his thigh, but that made it worse. 'Try saying your five times tables,' she suggested.

He started off fine, but got stuck after fifty. 'It's no use.'

'You lie down then,' Susan said. And when he was down on the floor she stood above him, one leg either side of his stiff cock, and squatted with her knees bent out, so her vulva was exposed above him. She closed her eyes and opened her bladder. She felt the stream of urine start on its course and knew that it was too late to stop. So she let herself go, she gave up all control, she surrendered totally . . . and out it gushed in a strong stream, spraying down on him, splashing against her own ankles. She shivered slightly at the sense of release, and then she enjoyed. She just let the feeling wash through her and out of her, out of her urethra, and she relished it. She gyrated her hips to broadcast the golden shower, and then tilted her pelvis backwards so the stream shot up on to the boy's chest. And as the flow slowed she actively pushed the reserve out, enjoying herself to the last drop.

Finally she opened her eyes. The boy's cock was stiffer than ever.

'It's not fair,' Susan grumbled. 'You're not keeping your part of the deal.' But just telling him off wasn't enough somehow. With a flash of inspiration she reached for the hose and turned it on. He seemed powerless to move beneath her. She resumed her position astride his middle and held the hose between her bottom cheeks, the nozzle just below her vulva. Cold water streamed out of her crotch in a torrent and he gasped and squirmed. Again she moved her hips, drenching him all over. At last he wriggled off his back and struggled on to his hands and knees. Then she took the hose in one hand, about three feet from the end, and lashed his bottom with it, giggling. He objected playfully, but his attempts to deny her a good target seemed strangely ineffective and they frolicked wildly until matron told them it was time for the next players.

'Roll up! Roll up! Three darts for a good lick!'

Goode sauntered over to Jill's and Jane's, where trade

was drying up. They were offering a bonus incentive: 'Stick all three on your target and you can choose which of its caverns of delight you want to take your prize in!'

They tossed to decide who would serve Goode, and Jane won. Jill insisted that she would enjoy watching so much, she didn't mind at all.

Both women were naked except for a mass of flowers in their hair and thin cotton skirts which came down to their ankles. Jane stood in front of Goode at the barrier, turned to face away from him, and touched her toes. Jill stood alongside, facing Goode, and grasped the fabric of Jane's skirt halfway down. She pulled it up slowly, as though revealing the crown jewels.

Goode let out an appreciative sigh, which turned to a gasp as Jane's bottom was finally exposed. It was dotted with bright red hickeys and tiny love bites.

'Kilroy was here,' Jill explained boastfully. 'Mine's the same. I think they like paying for the darts as much as winning a prize.'

With his tongue, Goode thoroughly wet a large area on each of Jane's cheeks. She walked away from him five paces and touched her toes again. He licked the rubber sucker on the end of his dart and took aim.

The first shot was a bull's eye, right on the mid-line slit, and the dart fell unkissed to the ground. The second shot hit the rounded flesh of the left buttock, but at a bit of an angle, and it too fell. Jill grabbed Jane by the hips and pulled her back two paces towards Goode. His third dart smacked in place and quivered to a proud halt on her right cheek.

Jill waved Goode forward. She pulled the sucker off with another smacking sound and quiver of flesh, and taking Goode's erect cock in one hand, she guided it skilfully beneath her friend's buttocks, between her labia, and into her vagina.

Jill knelt, one hand around Jane's thigh and the other stroking the back of Goode's, and watched the smooth pumping action close-up. It was a perfect fit, like a piston in an engine cylinder, in and out, in and out, the piston glistening with lubricant, the cylinder with synchronised timing rising and falling, rising to meet it and falling away, with miles to go and miles to go . . .

Until the flower lady interrupted, with flowers for them all and a warning that others wanted a go, and he'd had a fair turn.

There were flowers on everyone now, and not much clothing. Plenty of people were stark naked except for their flowers. And some of them were wreathed in garlands.

Even Carnel's former squaw had earned a crown of daisies, which she wore with joy on her jet-black hair above the glory of her nakedness. Ella checked by the stocks to see how she was doing and found a small line of ladies waiting by her side. They had set a table in front of the stocks, with a chair on it facing the captive face, and took it in turns sitting on the chair with their legs up over the top of the stocks to bring their vulvas into contact with Carnel's mouth.

'He was a bit reluctant at first,' the squaw reported. 'And a bit rough, too. But with a little guidance from my moccasin on his big bad bum he's come along wonderfully.'

'You'd think he'd never feel it through all that blubber,' Ella said.

'He's just a big fat crybaby.'

A chubby woman waiting in line winked at Ella. 'But it's the big fat ones that can really get to you, if they give it a bit of welly. He's got the best technique on the field.'

And perhaps it was true, because even Blas Carnel, fully dressed and locked in place, was sporting half a dozen splendid dahlias, stuffed into his pockets in recognition of his contribution.

The entire village green had been transformed into a floral, pagan, exuberant, joyful temple of sexual intensity.

And some of the fantasies which Ella and Goode had laid down blossomed in delightfully varied forms and hybrids.

The fiddle-player with the morris men, for instance, had turned the musical chairs game into a bawdy country dance, with himself as caller. As Ella passed he roped her in because there was a man without a partner. A cricketer. *The* cricketer. The Saxon hulk. She couldn't resist.

'Take your partner by the cock!' the fiddler called.

'Ladies with your partner's cock in your right hand . . . Gents with your left hand on your partner's bottom . . . you can tickle her if you like. Now lead him round in a big circle to the left, ladies . . . one . . . two . . .' And he launched into a lively rendition of Lord Fazakerly's reel.

'Now spin your partner by the cock . . .

'Pump your partner, one, two, three . . .

'Now pat her bum, gents, and pass her on . . .

'Take your new partner in the same ol' hold and back again the other way . . .'

Damn! She'd lost the hulk already! But the music was infectious, and this new morris cock was a delight to hold.

'Now gents take a seat and ladies dance on . . . and when the music pauses, sit on the nearest lap.' He played himself into a frenzy and Ella skipped ahead enthusiastically, or dawdled enthusiastically, depending on where she was in the circle in relation to the Saxon dick.

The music stopped, and Ella was ninety degrees out. She flopped down on the morris cock in front of her, facing inwards, and watched with glee as Susan, dallying as if to avoid it, was obliged to accept that she had drawn the hulk. Ella bobbed up and down on her morris man as the little darling backed into the lap of the cricketer with the biggest bat. At the last minute a dainty little hand reached under the dainty little bottom, delicately fingered the enormous cock, and steered it into the sweet descending cunt. Ella came, helplessly, at the sight of it. And thinking this was perhaps not sporting, she kept bobbing up and down on the cock between her own legs as though tapping her foot in time to the music.

'On your feet again,' the caller shouted as he switched to a polka. 'And take your partner in a ballroom hold.' There was a moment's muddle and he had to make himself clearer: 'That means open your legs, ladies, and make room for the balls . . . That's it, up on your toes if you need to . . . And off we go!'

Goode, too, found an interesting mutation . . . at the feely box. You went round the back of a stall, where *two* hand-sized holes, three feet apart, had been cut in the canvas. Little black sleeves had been attached, so you couldn't see what you were touching.

Feeling his way gingerly, Goode slid his hands into both sleeves simultaneously, and as soon as he made contact with flesh, a torrent of vulgar words descended on him from both sides.

'Cock . . . dong . . . whanger . . . knob head!'

And knob head it undoubtedly was, right and left.

'Stiffy . . . smeggy . . . cocksucker . . .'

The feely-boxers had amalgamated with the talk-dirties.

'Wank, suck, fuck . . .'

'Spunk, balls, cum, jism . . .'

The words spat down on him like machine-gun bullets. And yet the objects in his hands felt so warm and kindly. He ran his fingers over the domelike glans, peeping one finger tip into each little hole at the very top. He curled around the rims, screwing gently one way and then the other, then slid his hands down, grasping the whole of each shaft in his palms, wrapping all his fingers round, and stroking the skin up and down, up and down. The words came slower, softer. More like a spud gun. Then he reached the balls, covered with down, and he cupped them, and stroked again, as gently as he would the throat of a kitten. The words came floating down like bubbles.

And then the cocks were gone. He heard a shuffling of feet and withdrew his hands. He filled his lungs with the good night air and was about to head towards the music and dancing when he heard two disgruntled female voices.

'Come on then, punters, give us a feel!'

He looked around him. There was no one else within hearing.

'Punters meet cunters . . . come on, feel somethin' luvvly!'

He stepped back and slid his hands into the two black holes.

'Ooh, aah! . . . wet fucking mantrap! Luvvly wet cunt slopping in cuntjuice and full of sperm . . . one man's sperm and another man's spunk . . . a larder full of cunt . . . Give me more fingers!'

The other felt more oily, and at first he couldn't find the opening.

'Oh, you beast! In you go! Oh you bugger! Bugger! Bugger!'

Goode noticed the moon for the first time, rising as big as a dinner plate, white as china clay, over the roofs of the village. It was getting late.

The caller bowed out of his role with a formation so beautiful that others stopped to watch, and then joined in. He lay everyone down in a huge circle and hooked them together, mouth-to-cock and cunt-to-mouth. As more joined, there were a few gay hiccups in the male-female-male-female chain, but the circle stayed linked, by mouth and genitals, and it seemed to generate a cooperative spirit which eased this lovely orgy of sex into a more concentrated frame of mind. Each link in the chain started sucking up a storm.

Many of the flowers scattered around the field denoted orgasms of one kind or another. Some men had already ejaculated more than once, and some women had come in multiples. But all had kept something big in reserve . . . a climax for *the* climax. Now Ella walked around the circle, stroking here, patting there, and whispering endearments and encouragement. Some broke away from the circle and joined her in the middle; the others closed ranks and brought themselves and their partners close to the brink.

Ella caught Goode's hand and pulled him towards her. They kissed, and held each other close. Susan was nearby, with the music-loving cricketer, and Jane with the Saxon hulk. Jill had teemed up with the schoolmaster, and the squaw with his nephew. And Lallie, still in her stilettos, stockings and basque, had lost her congressman after all and had picked up an adoring adolescent scorekeeper.

Goode knelt and kissed Ella's breasts. Ella knelt and kissed Goode's cock. Then she lay down on the good rich earth and opened her legs. He knelt between them and with the tip of his penis he kissed her labia, kissed her clitoris. As he lowered his naked body down on hers, stomach to stomach and chest on breasts, he brought his mouth down on hers in a deep French kiss and slid his penis deep into her vagina.

Everyone inside the circle was fucking. Everyone was bringing themselves close to the brink.

Ella wrapped her legs around Goode's and they fucked each other. She rocked from side to side. She breathed in the energy which was swirling so strongly around her, she rose on it, and she breathed out enriched and enriching. They rose higher together, closer together, thrusting and absorbing; the very earth beneath them thrust upwards, absorbing until, when Ella opened her eyes, everything in her field of vision, like everything in her field of sensation, seemed to tremble and vibrate. Even the bells . . .

The church clock chimed and then began to strike the hours of midnight.

The vibrations rose to breaking point as hips thrust and grasped and throats cried out in agitation . . . agitation and ecstasy . . . fucking fucking fucking . . . to the very last stroke, the very last stroke . . . until all effort exploded into exhaustless, limitless bliss and a glorious happy energy that was pure unbridled sex swept from them and enveloped all. It invested the green, the tower and its bells, the village, the county . . . it enveloped the entire world, the skies, moon, stars, cosmos . . .

And when Ella opened her eyes again, after her own orgasmic explosion, she saw what looked like a shooting star dropping through the skies above her. It blazed a shining trail for two desperate seconds and then burst into a frenzy of sparks. And then it went dark, and Ella knew they had fucked Carnel's satellite to oblivion.

By the light of day it was discovered that a narrow ring of scorched earth had appeared around the edge of the green in Pod Parva, along the course of the recently installed drainage system, and nothing over the ensuing weeks and months would induce grass to grow there. And yet in a smaller circle within it, about the size you would get if sixty or so people lay round head to toe, but overlapping a little, the grass seemed to grow with more vigour and a deeper, richer colour. And for years to come, no matter how often it was mowed, it always sported a wonderful abundance of flora, whether swathes of bright buttercups and sunny daisies or singular wild orchids.

And though a detailed memory of the events of that night was wiped from the consciousness of the villagers by the same stroke of renewal which restored their normal, healthy appetite for sex, it is certainly the case that Pod Parva has about it an aura of generous, joyful sexuality which is far from typical.

The village green is the focus of this charm. There lovers enjoy themselves in exploration and celebration of the sensual, unrestrained by the censure of their neighbours. From courting adolescents to rejuvenated octogenarians, you will see them openly enjoying their hugs and kisses. They pet quite heavily on the bench donated by a congressman from the New World who fell in love with this congenial corner of the old. And among those who like, occasionally, to go the whole way under the stars, it is an open secret that there is a very convenient and lovely little dip, where the pond used to be.

13

TO EACH THEIR ISLE

Ella smoothed Goode's hair from his forehead and planted a little kiss above the bridge of his nose before collapsing on the bed beside him. He turned on his side so that he stayed inside her, and cradled her shoulders in the crook of his arm.

'I think after all this,' Goode said, 'I need a little retreat . . . a spot of quiet bird-watching by myself somewhere. There's a little island in Micronesia that might do fine . . .'

Ella snuggled up against his chest, taking care to grip his resting member and keep a hold on him. She had worked him almost as hard during the days since the fête as she had that momentous night. Though he had played his part as her wordsmith superbly:

'Come to bed with me . . .

'Let's do it again . . .

'The night is young . . .'

They had moved from her cottage at one end of The Row to his at the other; from his bed back to hers. To Goode she seemed overflowing with a beautiful generous strength.

'You smile like a bouquet of roses . . .

'Your skin is as smooth as a rose petal . . .

'When I smell you, it's like breathing roses . . .'

And in these blissful village days, Ella had felt as though she were truly at home. She had basked in the physical and spiritual glory of an English paradise on earth, in a perfect English June, with a gorgeous English man. She felt that she had reclaimed a crucial part of her inheritance. But she too was aware that it was time to be moving on.

'And I know just the right little island for me,' she answered Goode. 'An absolute deadwater compared to Pod Parva. It's called Manhattan.'

She felt a tiny surge inside her, a little pulse of surprise from his nodding penis. She stretched her hand up and kissed Goode on the side of his neck. She wet the end of her tongue and traced the folds of his ear. She nibbled the soft flesh of the lobe. Then she pursed her tongue and gently penetrated his delicate hearing orifice, blowing softly around it at the same time. His penis lurched.

Ella rolled on top of him again, sitting with one knee on either side of his hips, and slowly rocked her pelvis up and down until she had drawn him back into a full erection. And then she launched into a little fun on his chest. She kissed his nipples into their cute little stiffness, and then with her lips cushioning her teeth she bit them. She licked a little patch of hair and when it was thoroughly wet, curled and twisted it between her fingers, and tugged. She pushed his arms up above his head and repeated her play, first under one arm and then in the pit of the other. When he tried to roll her back on to the bed she leaned down on him, squashing her breasts on his chest, and stretched her hands forward above his head. She ran them down his arms until they met his hands, and curled their fingers together.

Goode began thrusting his pelvis up against hers. Ella slid her feet down his legs until her two soft insteps pressed against the arch of his feet. She pushed down with her feet and up with her hands, stretching them both. She was entirely supported by his body now, their flesh in contact from fingertip to toe.

He took her by surprise, rolling both of their bodies over in a quick firm move so that their positions were exactly reversed. And then with a lock of his swept-back hair falling down over his eyes he pumped his cock in her with furious abandon, hurtling towards another climax.

At the very last moment Ella caught him off guard in turn, and swung them back again. She followed through by lifting her chest up on her arms, and she kept the pumping motion going by swiftly raising and lowering her cunt and fucking him actively herself. His ejaculation was assured, she could tell by his sense of surrender. She rubbed her clitoris hard against his pubic bone. It was so easy to come quickly in this position, once she was hot. And it seemed with Goode that she was *always* hot.

Greedy to absorb the sensuality of their orgasm as fully as they could, both of them strained their necks and looked down, between their bodies, at the conjunction of their sexual organs. Ella's breasts drooped voluptuously, their nipples just grazing the hair on Goode's chest. Through the gap of her cleavage they both watched her cunt rise and fall, exposing and then swallowing up the thick, glistening shaft of his cock. She rose higher, to see more of it. Then she sank down until the rich auburn hair above her sex mingled with the darker, wiry hair above his.

They watched transfixed as they fucked. And then both of them giggled as her cunt collapsed juddering like a deflating balloon around the piercing stimulus which was his cock slamming out its sperm.

Ella smoothed Goode's hair from his forehead and planted a little kiss above the bridge of his nose before collapsing on the bed beside him. He turned on his side so that he stayed inside her, and cradled her shoulders in the crook of his arm.

There was just one more loose end to tie up before they fled the sceptred isle.

Ella had already invited Toni back for a pleasant lunch and a few explanations amidst a mutual exchange of thanks. She had thought that she would have need of Higgins and Son to dig up the orgone-piping around the green. And in one of her more ambitious scenarios she would have induced them to relay the pipes secretly, perhaps inside old field drains located from their ancient archives, around Pod Manor. But in the event, the same overload of orgone energy which had blown the SMIPT satellite out of the sky had vaporised the pipes around the green. And via a defecting squaw, Ella had learned that it also melted the entire stockpile at Pod Magna and blew up the research lab at Pod Manor. 'Quite an evening,' Toni said. 'Yet darling son of Higgins never even got to grips with *my* piping!'

And Ella had received a lovely thank-you card from Melissa on behalf of the three chums. She said they were getting their treat-of-a-lifetime, all-expenses-paid trip to the States after all, courtesy not of Blas Carnel and SMIPT but the triumvirate he had brought along that fêteful night. While her religious broadcaster was indulging himself in the water-sports tent, Melissa had sneaked out her pocket camera and captured the moment for posterity. She enclosed a handful of candid snapshots. So the influential Americans, who were to become Carnel's insurance policy, became Ella's instead.

The very last caller at her country cottage was coming the furthest and was to give Ella the greatest satisfaction.

Ted the Village Stores brought him from the airstrip at Pod Magna, and he shuffled through her back door with a nod and a handshake and no time for the roses, like a minor official on a trade mission to the third world. He plonked a Gladstone bag on the kitchen table and rushed into his business as if aiming to be out of there before the dust settled.

'The deeds to an apartment on Central Park, in your name, Ella.' He dropped a wad of papers in front of her. 'And the keys.' There was a jingle of metal, followed by more documents. 'A bank account with a handsome allowance to be paid annually. And all the major credit cards.'

Ella smiled. 'The pay-off.'

The man made no comment. He took a pen from his inside pocket and was marking various places for Ella to sign, when Goode sauntered downstairs from the bedroom.

'You!' he exclaimed.

'You already know my guardian angel?' Ella asked, without much surprise.

'This is the man who first suggested I come to Pod Parva. I thought he was a journalist, working for my father!'

'He works for my step-father,' Ella said. 'But no doubt your daddy knows my daddy, or my family's firm owes your family's firm or something . . . global village and all that . . .'

The lawyer-guardian hastily scooped back the forms which Ella signed.

'I don't know what SMIPT stands for,' she continued. 'But whether the T is for Texas or Telecommunications, you can bet my friend here is very interested in what they're up to. You can be sure he's got his spies, his industrial espionage team. And when all else failed, you can be damn certain he wouldn't hesitate to send in two blind moles like us.'

The man snapped his bag shut and stood up to leave.

'And the idea worked, didn't it?' Ella said. 'Better than he can possibly have expected. On the morning of the fête I even stole into the SMIPT yard in Pod Magna and cut off a sample length of orgone pipe.'

The man stopped halfway to the door. 'You did?'

'I thought to myself: the piping itself isn't bad, just because SMIPT put it to such evil use. I thought, Wilhelm Reich used his orgone boxes in therapy, to heal people. Just think what he could have done with a box made out of this stuff!'

The man put his bag on the floor and sat down again.

'The trouble is, George, my guardian here has been a bit naughty.' She tried to put herself back in his office that day when it all began, to remember the details, to mimic them. 'In fact he's been a very naughty little boy indeed.'

'Well, perhaps I wasn't as straightforward as I could have been.'

Ella took a sheaf of black and white prints from a drawer. The walk-in larder in Goode's cottage had made a super darkroom and Ted had soon located the essential equipment. The hours in between making love with Goode had been spent with her second love.

There was a shot of a dull cricketer raising his bat aimlessly; a lifeless woman pulling flower petals apart; someone half-heartedly poking at a milestone with a walking stick. They pictured a soulless acting-out of monotonous tradition.

'Come on,' Ella said. 'Let's see what you've got under that grim business suit you're wearing. Chose it specially for gloomy old England, did you?'

'Ella, you can't mean it! I'm your guardian!'

'One spank for every sexless scene you tricked me into.'

'But that was just a little game,' he pleaded.

'What is life but a string of little games?' She paused deliciously. 'And now it's my turn to play.'

'But you enjoyed it!'

'Up to a point, if I remember correctly, guardian mine. Only up to a point.'

Now he looked torn. Ella reached over and put her hand against his crotch. Whether the thrill came from the prospect of returning with a certain length of pipe, or something else, she felt a growing bulge.

'You cut a piece of the pipe off?' he asked, nervously checking the stakes.

'I cut off a piece of the pipe.'

He stood and took off his jacket, hanging it neatly over the back of the chair. Then his tie. He unfastened the top button of his shirt and stretched out his neck.

Ella said, 'Cut the theatrics.'

He resigned himself to his fate and hastily took off his shirt, tossing it carelessly over the chair; prised his shoes off by the heel without unfastening the laces; and pushed down his trousers and underwear together, leaving them in a heap on top of his shoes.

'You can leave the socks,' Ella said. 'They're rather cute.'

In fact his whole body was rather cute, Ella thought. He had a bit of a paunch, but there was a tantalising strip of dark close hair running over it, from the thick bush of his pubes to the forest on his chest, and it elevated the rising contour into a sensual feature. She would have liked to run her fingers along it, and to nip little bits of surplus flesh between her thumb and forefinger. But she kept her purpose firmly in mind and asked Goode to tie the man's ankles together with a leather thong she had ready for the purpose.

The man stood compliantly, and Ella knew that he would enjoy the little charade to be played out on his bottom. If she let him.

'Right then, hands off.'

He moved his hands from in front of his cock and it stood to attention like a soldier, spick and span and ready for action. Ella gave Goode two more long strips of leather. He tied one end of each around a wrist, and passed the other ends through two enormous hooks which were screwed into the thick black beam running across the ceiling.

'Just like a pair of hams,' Ella said, when the thongs had been pulled tight and secured. Her guardian was stretched with his hands apart and above so his body formed a Y, and his cock showed all the signs of loving it.

So Ella filled a bucket with cold water. She pushed the table to one side and then without giving him time to anticipate, hurled the water at his midriff.

The little line of sexy hair became a sooty rivulet, and then it clung, straight and jet black, to his skin. And the cock, after one quick lurch like a gasp for air, retreated willy-nilly, right back to base. While Goode floundered around the wet floor telling himself to stop trying to work out what Ella was up to, and just enjoy the event as theatre, Ella grabbed hold of the shrivelled-up cock and pushed it back between her guardian's legs.

'Get the belt, in that drawer!'

Ella pointed. And eager not to appear insubordinate in front of someone he presumed to be a common adversary, Goode obeyed. It was a sort of jockstrap with extra bits, as though it had been made for Siamese twins.

'I borrowed it from Toni,' Ella said. 'She showed me how she used it.'

Ella was keeping the little willy pulled back hard, so no blood could flow back in and make it stiff, so she had to make use of Goode's hands too.

'Tie that bit round his waist. Good. Now pull his cheeks apart a bit.' She bent the penis round as far as it would go, tucking it up his bottom.

'You're squashing his balls,' Goode said. 'Try it one side or the other.'

She eased it hard left and tucked it in again.

'Close his bottom! Hold his cheeks shut! Damn, it's squiggled out.'

It mushroomed to the next size up. But she jerked it back mercilessly.

'Now! Pull that cord tight . . . Wrap that flap round his balls . . .'

Ella's guardian sought dignity in silence.

And within ten minutes they had his cock strapped up so there was no way he could get an erection.

Ella moved the table back. Then she pushed it even further, against the place where her guardian's cock would have been, ordinarily. He shuffled back. She pushed further. He shuffled back again. But his hands were still secure in their hooks, so this movement had the effect of stretching him out even more. Now he was up on his toes, he was bent at the crotch, and his bottom was sticking out behind him. Ella saw him counting the pictures.

'There are eight,' she said. She handed Goode a cane and said, 'Give him twelve. Nice and slow.'

The man opened his mouth to protest.

'Lawyers can't count anyway,' Ella said. The man stuck to his policy of dignity and closed his mouth.

After the first few strokes of the cane Ella pulled another sheaf of prints from her drawer and scattered them on the table, on top of the others. Her guardian was distracted temporarily from the impact on his bottom. Here were two men playing bells on a pair of close-up breasts. There was a man sandwiched between two gorgeous women, naked except for flowers.

'I did cut off a piece of the orgone pipe,' Ella said after the sixth or seventh stroke of the cane. 'But it vaporised too, along with all the rest. It really was too bad. It left a nasty stain in my bag.'

The man was speechless. Dignity didn't have anything to do with it. Had Ella looked at him, she might have felt some compassion. At the very least she would have kissed that darling snake of black hair curling round his navel. But she had been drawn into her own photographs. As she looked at the shot of Susan helping to petal the mermaid's fanny, she remembered the feel of her tiny hot nipples on the wet grass the night the well-dressing was erected. And she started to rub her crotch, through her dress, against the edge of the table.

Ella rubbed harder as she shuffled the prints . . . the captain ordering his cricketers to a closer field, his eye full of sudden vital passion for the game . . . and she pictured herself there on the pitch, on her back, feeling the Saxon hulk drive his dick inside her as she watched ten other cocks flailing in the air above her.

Her guardian started to moan, perhaps from the impact of the cane, perhaps from the vision before him. It was rich in longing, with an overtone of regret. Without looking up, Ella leaned forward a little to bring her clitoris into better contact with the table.

Here was the adolescent struggling to scramble over her hiking boots – how on earth had she got into that position? – and getting his thin wiry penis trapped in the process. And here was another dick, a great big monument of a dick, smeared with strawberry tart and globs of thick cream . . .

She was vaguely aware that the caning was over. The moaning had changed in tone, had become strangely more insistent. But she couldn't tear her eyes off her photographs.

And then she felt the skirt of her dress being lifted from the rear. It was lifted all the way up, to her waist. She felt Goode's hands on her knickerless hips. Ella kept on rubbing her clitoris gently up and down against the edge of the table as Goode's penis probed the slit between her cheeks.

'Ah! Oh! Let me free, I want to fuck . . .'

Now it was Ella and Goode who kept their dignity through silence.

'I want to wank! Let me wank . . .'

Goode's cock jabbed exploratorily beneath the underhang of Ella's bottom.

'I need to stretch! I want to be stiff! Just let me get hard! . . .'

The rosy tip of the cock struck moisture. It dipped inside the engorged lips of her cunt to wet itself and then it slid effortlessly deep inside.

Ella felt full. She felt full and happy and at home, with Manhattan and the rest of her life before her. The cock inside her pumped in and out and in and out. She gently pushed her bottom backwards to meet it and started fucking back. She looked up at her lawyer-guardian and smiled.

HELP US TO PLAN THE FUTURE OF EROTIC FICTION –

– and no stamp required!

The Nexus Library is Britain's largest and fastest-growing collection of erotic fiction. We'd like your help to make it even bigger and better.

Like many of our books, the questionnaire below is completely anonymous, so don't feel shy about telling us what you really think. We want to know what kind of people our readers are – we want to know what you like about Nexus books, what you dislike, and what changes you'd like to see.

Just answer the questions on the following pages in the spaces provided; if more than one person would like to take part, please feel free to photocopy the questionnaire. Then tear the pages from the book and send them in an envelope to the address at the end of the questionnaire. No stamp is required.

THE NEXUS QUESTIONNAIRE

SECTION ONE: ABOUT YOU

1.1 Sex *(yes, of course, but try to be serious for just a moment)*
    Male ☐   Female ☐

1.2 Age
    under 21 ☐   21 – 30 ☐
    31 – 40 ☐   41 – 50 ☐
    51 – 60 ☐   over 60 ☐

1.3 At what age did you leave full-time education?
    still in education ☐   16 or younger ☐
    17 – 19 ☐   20 or older ☐

1.4 Occupation _____

1.5 Annual household income
    under £10,000 ☐   £10–£20,000 ☐
    £20–£30,000 ☐   £30–£40,000 ☐
    over £40,000 ☐

1.6 Where do you live?
Please write in the county in which you live (for example Hampshire), or the city if you live in a large metropolitan area (for example Manchester) _____

SECTION TWO : ABOUT BUYING NEXUS BOOKS

2.1 How did you acquire this book?
   I bought it myself ☐   My partner bought it ☐
   I borrowed it / found it ☐

2.2 If this book was bought ...
   ... in which town or city? _____
   ... in what sort of shop: High Street bookshop ☐
                               local newsagent ☐
                               at a railway station ☐
                               at an airport ☐
                               at motorway services ☐
                      other: _____

2.3 Have you ever had difficulty finding Nexus books on sale?
   Yes ☐   No ☐
   If you have had difficulty in buying Nexus books, where would you like to be able to buy them?
   ... in which town or city _____
   ... in what sort of shop from
       list in previous question _____

2.4 Have you ever been reluctant to buy a Nexus book because of the sexual nature of the cover picture?
   Yes ☐   No ☐

2.5 Please tick which of the following statements you agree with:
   I find some Nexus cover pictures offensive /
      too blatant ☐

   I would be less embarassed about buying Nexus
      books if the cover pictures were less blatant ☐

   I think that in general the pictures on Nexus books
      are about right ☐

   I think Nexus cover pictures should be as sexy
      as possible ☐

SECTION THREE: ABOUT NEXUS BOOKS

3.1 How many Nexus books do you own? _____

3.2 Roughly how many Nexus books have you read? _____

3.3 What are your three favourite Nexus books?
    First choice _____
    Second Choice _____
    Third Choice _____

3.4 What are your three favourite Nexus cover pictures?
    First choice _____
    Second choice _____
    Third choice _____

SECTION FOUR: ABOUT YOUR IDEAL EROTIC NOVEL

We want to publish books you want to read – so this is your chance to tell us exactly what your ideal erotic novel would be like.

4.1 Using a scale of 1 to 5 (1 = no interest at all, 5 = your ideal), please rate the following possible settings for an erotic novel:
    - Medieval/barbarian/sword 'n' sorcery ☐
    - Renaissance/Elizabethan/Restoration ☐
    - Victorian/Edwardian ☐
    - 1920s & 1930s – the Jazz Age ☐
    - Present day ☐
    - Future/Science Fiction ☐

4.2 Using the same scale of 1 to 5, please rate the following styles in which an erotic novel could be written:
    - Realistic, down to earth, set in real life ☐
    - Escapist fantasy, but just about believable ☐
    - Completely unreal, impressionistic, dreamlike ☐

4.3 Would you prefer your ideal erotic novel to be written from the viewpoint of the main male characters or the main female characters?
    Male ☐   Female ☐

4.4 Is there one particular setting or subject matter that your ideal erotic novel would contain?
    _____

SECTION FIVE: LAST WORDS

5.1 What do you like best about Nexus books?

_____

_____

5.2 What do you most dislike about Nexus books?

_____

_____

5.3 In what way, if any, would you like to change Nexus covers?

_____

_____

5.4 Here's a space for any other comments:

_____

_____

_____

_____

_____

_____

Thank you for completing this questionnaire. Now tear it out of the book – carefully! – put it in an envelope and send it to:

**Nexus Books
FREEPOST
London
W10 5BR**

No stamp is required.